The chugging retort alerted the last gunner

But by then it was too late. Bolan nailed the shadow in the chest, flinging him into the brush.

"Striker to Flyboy," Bolan called over his handheld radio, "come in. I've been blown. Fly in and let it rip."

"Affirm—"

The Executioner heard a sudden silence on the other end, then the clear sound of the handle on a submachine gun being cocked.

The soldier's worst suspicions about Culmore became reality as Jack Grimaldi said, "Culmore, you want to tell me why you have your Uzi pointed at me?"

The transmission abruptly ended.

MACK BOLAN ®
The Executioner

DON PENDLETON'S
THE EXECUTIONER®
ASSAULT REFLEX

A GOLD EAGLE BOOK FROM
WORLDWIDE®

TORONTO • NEW YORK • LONDON
AMSTERDAM • PARIS • SYDNEY • HAMBURG
STOCKHOLM • ATHENS • TOKYO • MILAN
MADRID • WARSAW • BUDAPEST • AUCKLAND

First edition March 1999
ISBN 0-373-64243-1

Special thanks and acknowledgment to
Dan Schmidt for his contribution to this work.

ASSAULT REFLEX

No punishment has ever possessed enough power
of deterrence to prevent the commission of crimes.
—Hannah Arendt
1906–1975

Change the land, the culture, the language and still
the one constant is organized crime. Whatever
mask of legitimacy it wears, it is still Animal Man
at its worst. I will unmask this menace and stamp it
out at every turn, its final deterrent.
—Mack Bolan

For keepers of the peace, everywhere

1

Over the Arabian Sea

Petre Kuschka pointed the muzzle of a 9 mm Makarov between Ben Calhoun's eyes.

If the ex-KGB assassin squeezed the pistol's trigger, then Calhoun knew all his dreams of glory and living as a god among mere mortals would surely die. Desire for the good life, even if it came at the expense of countless innocent lives, was a strange thing to experience right then. But he couldn't deny it was there, as fleeting as it was. All he had worked and hungered for, sweated over and killed for, forsaking God and country, betraying his oath to the United States government, leaving himself wide open to termination with extreme prejudice at the hands of Uncle Sam's black-operations agents, gone quite possibly in the next heartbeat, and for what? Why?

Vast wealth, unbridled pleasure and ultimate rule over the Third World nation of his choosing, suddenly became the least of the concerns of the former U.S. Special Forces major. Grim reality stared him down. Living through the next few seconds took top priority.

The black snout of the pistol didn't waver a fraction of an inch from its target point. A strange and horrible smile then danced over the lips of Petre

Kuschka. The Russian bastard, Calhoun thought, had him dead to rights and was playing it out. Was Kuschka trying to make him sweat out a confession of some wrongdoing or personal conspiracy against the Coalition? Did the Russian blame Calhoun and his men for the disasters that had plagued and dogged them halfway around the world? Did Kuschka think Calhoun was playing some treacherous game for personal gain?

The Americans had just as much to lose as their Russian counterparts. They were all in so deep now, being hunted by unknown enemies from country to country, continent to continent, their collective butts kicked so hard wherever they went the ranks were thinned now to a skeleton force. There was no turning back their own machine of death and destruction they had planned to unleash in the forms of biological, chemical and nuclear blackmail.

"Clearly we've got a problem here," Calhoun said, not sure if he was stalling until he could make his own move, or looking to talk his way out of sure death. Whatever, Calhoun could taste the fear in his dry mouth, felt the sweat run cold down the back of his neck. From the corner of his eye, Calhoun could see what was left of his own soldiers, that skeleton force of eight men, his people braced on the edge of their seats, fists wrapped around M-16s or Uzis, ready to go down with the ship. And if the bullets started flying at twenty thousand feet in the air...

Kuschka was flanked by his own former-Spetsnaz troops, all of whom had AK-47s leveled on the Americans. Just beyond Kuschka, four Pakistanis lay in their pooling blood where the Russians had executed them only moments earlier. The word had just come in, apparently, that the freighter that had left Karachi with their plutonium, uranium and other nuclear component parts had been boarded and seized by the U.S. military. There had been a leak or an informant, and it was all going to hell. Again.

Obviously the news of their latest setback had set off the time bomb in Kuschka, and a moment of truth had arrived. Russians against Americans, East meets West. The cold war was on the verge of turning hot. A gun battle with assault rifles blazing away right then was certain suicide. One round through the cabin's wall or a window and the whole aircraft would rip apart, bodies sailing out into the infinite darkness with only the cold ocean at the end of free fall. So much for dreams of world conquest. Goodbye dominion over the weaker and inferior elements of the human race. So long rewards for so much blood and sweat, tribulation and trial by hellfire. Of course, the Hydra Project would march on. But without the frontline troops, it would take some time, Calhoun wanted to believe, for the Coalition to regroup, reorganize. Then again, maybe not. Something warned the former major this thing was bigger than him or his Russian comrades. All of them were expendable in the bigger scheme.

Dreams aside, it was pure survival reflex, coupled with a hard-edged go-to-hell mind-set, that made Calhoun drop his hand over the barrel of his AK-47. He had faced down his own death and walked away too many times with the blood of his enemies on his hands to go out with a whimper. Not even the wounded lion, he thought, simply crawled off into the bush to die.

"You'll never make it," Kuschka warned.

"You won't, either."

Kuschka chuckled. "You are right, Major. We, indeed, have a serious problem here. All right. Let's everyone relax, take a deep breath."

"You first."

Kuschka smiled. "Convince me we are still on the same team."

Calhoun watched for a long, tense moment as Kuschka seemed to think about something. Waiting, Calhoun stared deep into the black eyes of the Russian killer, those bushy eyebrows that were nearly knit together, the jagged scars and dead tissue on Kuschka's face, inflicted from wars and killzones long since gone but not forgotten. Calhoun couldn't decide if Kuschka was a freak show or a fearsome sight of death incarnate. Weird thought, of course, to have when he was staring down his own end.

He had known the Russian killer since his days in Vietnam, where the two of them had decided to profit from a winless war, walk away with something for the future. The future had endured between them over the years, Calhoun connecting the then-KGB killer to CIA operations and counterintelligence in countries that most Americans probably didn't even know existed, much less cared about unless a Marine barracks was bombed by Islamic fanatics in a suicide attack. The past, though, had paved its way to the present, and hopefully, for the future. The cold war was over, yes, but the present stagnation where the West found its enemies beyond the Kremlin was merely a sleeping lion. What Calhoun knew was planned by renegade factions on both sides would possibly erupt World War III at worst, hold the free world hostage at best.

Finally Kuschka nodded and lowered the Makarov. The whine of the jet's engines seemed to shriek through the cabin. In Russian, Kuschka barked an order at his men. Relief washed over Calhoun when those assault rifles were lowered, no longer staring him down.

"Let me see if I read this right," Calhoun said. "Feel free to correct me if I'm wrong. You suspect I have something to do with us getting our asses kicked all over the world. You suspect I'm leading whoever is chasing us from one point to the next. You believe I've abandoned ship or have set you up from the beginning."

"Do I? Right now, Comrade Major, I am sure of very little. In a few short minutes, I will have to radio our sponsors and inform them we are being hunted to the ends of the earth by an unknown enemy. Two men, to be exact, incredible as it all seems. One attacks us from the ground while his comrade pilot drops the sky on us. They are well armed, well informed and they show up wherever we go, annihilating our forces, disrupting our plans. They have cost us dearly. In men, money and matériel. In short, I am sick and tired of running, of looking over my shoulder for these two shadows of death, wondering who is with me and who is against me."

"Okay, so what do we do about it? We keep on running or do we stand our ground the next time and finish it?"

Kuschka's gaze narrowed. "I will be honest with you, and I hope you will return me the courtesy. I have had my doubts about you since we lost the shipment of drugs off the coast of Colombia. My suspicions have deepened since. These unknown adversaries show up in France, then Germany, hounding us, killing at will, chasing us from Europe to Lebanon, where we encounter a force of what I believe were CIA black operatives. Then Pakistan, the same thing. My shipment of enriched plutonium and uranium seized by the U.S. military.

"Put yourself in my place. After all, Comrade Major, you are former U.S. military. You see where I'm headed with this line of inquiry? So, yes, moments ago I considered killing you and your men. However, I want to believe in you. I want to believe this is all just some bizarre coincidence that wherever we go these nameless enemies just show up."

"Think about it," Calhoun responded. "First of all, my ass is on the firing line, too, and my own people have been dropping like flies in the face of this unknown enemy. They, whoever the hell 'they' are, are sanctioned by somebody in the U.S. military—who, I don't know. They have superior intelligence, for one thing, and carte blanche to kick ass and take names for another. How we've been found out or how much they know—well, I'm as in the dark as you are. Again, I have lost plenty of my own men to these bastards, guys I trust and have known for twenty-five, thirty years, and yeah, guys I would shed a tear for over their deaths under other circumstances, so don't think I'm not feeling the sting.

"What's more, my people have sacrificed everything for the Coalition and the final goals of Hydra. Meaning, I can never go back to the United States, Europe, wherever, except to fly on to Russia with you and your people. In other words, I've hung it out there to the bitter or the sweet end, whichever, no strings, no questions, no going back. If you don't believe me, you think I've had something to do with the disasters that have followed us since South America, then go on, feel free to make your move.''

Instantly the tension returned with a razor's edge to the cabin. Calhoun was calling the moment, hoping against hope the Russian was simply trying to bluff his way through it. If Kuschka even twitched, though, Calhoun would bring up his AK-47, hold back the trigger and want nothing more than to see the Russians the first ones off and screaming for the vast blackness beyond when the plane came apart.

Kuschka chuckled. ''Very well, Major. I will accept matters for what they are—at the moment. A mystery. Be warned, however. Should I find out otherwise...''

''Understood. You'll do what you have to do.''

Kuschka was turning away, but Calhoun had to get the final word in. ''Comrade Kuschka.''

Calhoun met those black eyes with an unwavering icy stare. ''Now, you be warned. If you ever pull a weapon on me or my men again...''

He let it hang.

Nodding, Kuschka said, ''Fair enough. I am glad we have reached an understanding. By the way, to answer your previous question. Should we encounter this unknown opposition again, we—meaning all of us—will stand our ground and defeat them, and to the last man. Now, if you will excuse me, I suggest you get some rest while I radio our superiors and inform them of all the misfortune that has befallen us.''

Calhoun settled back in his seat but his hand never strayed more than a few inches from his AK-47. Rest was the last thing he would be getting. If he slept at all, it would be with one eye open. More than ever, he trusted the Russians about as far as he could spit.

Whatever, he knew all of their troubles were far from over. In fact he expected things to get far worse before they got better.

If they ever did.

And "worse" for any of them would be sudden death at the end of the line, wherever that was. The only guarantee from there on was that more of their people would be dying at the hands of the unknown enemy, especially after Kuschka gave the standing order to go down to the last man in the face of another enemy attack.

The hell with all his dreams, Calhoun decided. He was simply looking to survive.

2

Manila

Running from an unknown enemy, waiting for the next lightning bolt of disaster and death to strike from a clear blue sky, was no longer a viable option. And if he was dead, then of course he couldn't spend or squander on wild pleasure or bribe his way to safe haven with any of the millions of illicit dollars he had taken from the KGB or from the Colombian drug cartels during his years of service as a five-star general in the United States Army, culminating as head of counterintelligence inside the walls of the Pentagon.

William McBain was sleeping, but he was stirring suddenly, seeing the secret past colliding with a nightmarish present, all of it driving him toward an uncertain, if not terrifying future. He didn't want to see the past or the present in his sleep, which was his only escape these days from a brutal reality. Still, thoughts of secrecy and visions of distant black operations in which he had been involved streamed through his mind, cursing him with the sleep of the damned—burning and screaming and trapped in a private hell—rather than the sleep of a newborn infant he so desperately wanted.

In his subconscious he began to rack up fleeting

memories, knowing all about secrets inside secrets, clandestine missions sanctioned by Uncle Sam against foreign and domestic terrorists, the toppling of dictatorial and brutal Third World regimes by CIA black operations. Over the years he had been the architect of such operations, and also the jealous guardian of knowledge, that, if the American public at large shared, would mean not a single politician would be left standing in the hallowed halls of Capitol Hill or a uniform left wandering the Pentagon. He had headed Project Balkan during the cold war where he had handed over the heads of CIA operatives to KGB assassins on a silver platter for whopping fees from the Kremlin. In his dreams the countless faces of dead CIA agents he had betrayed came howling for vengeance out of the blackness.

Fade to another vision.

Long ago, many lifetimes ago, there was the S Plan, headed up by Pentagon-groomed biochem specialists, working in biohazard suits in underground labs in Utah and Nevada. Around the clock, slaving away on taxpayer dollars, these modern-day alchemists were finalizing the sorcerer's touch on a doomsday germ meant to sterilize the male populace of Third World nations in order to cut their birthrate and keep those "select" countries from overrunning the rest of the civilized world. Against his will, McBain saw the seas of starving women and children stretched out on arid soil, too weak to cry out, all the shriveled black mummies rotting beneath a blazing sun, countless skeleton figures stumbling around mud huts.

Visions of Third World Armageddon faded, and more secret and horrible knowledge then began to surface in his mind. He knew about Operation Sphinx where the CIA had been ready to launch a takeover of major Middle East oil fields when the sheikhs had jacked up the price of oil so high Americans were killing one another as they strung out their vehicles in endless lines at the gas pumps. He knew about CIA cocaine trafficking for arms in the lower Americas where plenty of guys on the home team grew rich while the inner cities became battle zones and gangs proliferated across the U.S.

Suddenly he saw himself running from a monstrous explosion. Fire screamed for him, and he could feel the terrible heat racing to eat him alive.

He ran, but went nowhere, the fire following with relentless fury.

No, sir, William McBain, former five-star general, was sick and tired of living in fear and paranoia, and he heard his mind screaming for release from the nightmare, to stop running. There was too much to live for, and dying didn't fit into his plans. In fact it was high time to bail, run like hell with whatever funds he had squirreled away within easy reach. At last count, he knew there was five million in American cash in the wall safe of his latest safehouse.

He tried to force himself awake, but he knew the worst was yet to come.

McBain wasn't sure if these were conscious thoughts of fleeing or were part of his own subconscious voice screaming in terror and pain as dreams of untold wealth and power turned to visions of blood, fire and bodies ripped apart by explosions that kept on roaring out of nowhere. All he wanted was to sleep, as peaceful as a lamb.

But, he was waking now, hard and fast, hearing strange voices speaking in a foreign tongue he rec-

ognized as Russian. Reality check, and reality was
damn ugly these days. Stirring some more, he felt the
sledgehammer of too much booze pounding in his
skull, tasted the stale bourbon and cigar smoke in his
mouth. Then, blessedly, he smelled the sweeter fra-
grance of one of the two young Filipina prostitutes he
had partied with the night before. Then he smelled
the sweat on his body and recognized the odor for
what it was. Fear.

McBain was fully awake now, but unable to shake
off the vestiges of all he had seen in his sleep. For
the past two nights he'd had the same recurring visions, with slight variation of enemies and intensity
of violence. Either way, the whole world was after
him: armies of enraged Colombian drug lords and
their henchmen, hunting him down; head-clothed figures grinning in his face as they praised God and
cursed him as the Great Satan before they squeezed
the trigger; smaller armies of CIA agents, lurking in
the shadows of every corner in nameless, dark city
streets around the world. He heard his name carried
on the wind, the muttered whispers of strange voices
of relentless pursuers. Or he saw faceless figures with
radio earpieces, dark unmarked vehicles chasing him
from city to city, finally surrounding him, pulling him
from his own vehicle, then slapping the cuffs on him.
He was thrown aboard a military plane bound for the
States, his captors cursing him as the great traitor,
wishing him the worst as he spent the rest of his life
in Leavenworth.

But worst of all, without fail every night he saw a
tall, dark stranger with ice blue eyes in his night-
mares. The tall, nameless gunman rolled out the fires
of destruction he had wreaked from the ground, with

his unknown ally blowing up the world around them from his gunship above. The dark stranger, armed to the teeth, mowed down his comrades in the Coalition as McBain scurried for his life like a hunted animal. Luckily, this night he was coming to without the final nightmare scenario.

Would his fear of sudden death at the hands of the tall, ice-eyed gunman ever end?

If nothing else, coming awake now freed him from the nightmare of the tall, dark stranger and his lean ally stalking him through the jungles, the high seas, the cities and the deserts all over the world.

Small consolation. His own world was going straight to hell, and he was helpless to stop it.

Indeed, his own dream was dying, quick and ugly, and all that was left was a living nightmare.

And hell was calling for him in the shadowy pursuit of two nameless people he had never laid eyes on before it started to come unraveled in New York.

Two days now he had stayed under lock and key in the sprawling suite of his penthouse, Kuschka's Spetsnaz watchdogs guarding him, bringing in the booze and food, the smokes and whores. The entire floor of the new high-rise was, of course, bought and paid for with a small fortune of his ill-gotten gains. And the top floor of the New Hotel Manila was supposed to be a safehouse.

McBain felt his eyelids cracking open, his mind tumbling with all the reasons why his suite was far from the safest place on the planet.

After all, he was a man without a country, a once trusted protector and servant of the American people, but a man who had long ago sold his soul to the KGB and the drug cartels. He was stuck in the treacherous gray zone between ally and enemy. Hell, going for himself had now certainly put his neck in the hangman's noose. And the dark stranger who had pursued him and his supposed allies halfway around the world was tightening the noose every minute, he feared. Then he became angry with himself, told himself to stand tall, face it down, take it on the chin. Perhaps it was time to stand his ground, fight back. He was a soldier, after all, with two wars and a fair amount of combat and killing behind him.

"Comrade General, kindly get up and get dressed. You have important visitors."

His head swimming in booze, McBain saw the tall shadow in black standing in the far corner of the room. It was one of the five nameless Russian goons Kuschka had sent to guard him while he holed up in Manila, waiting for God only knew what.

McBain found his bed empty of the young women, briefly wondered how and when they had been whisked out of his bed. He looked at the drawn curtains, found the room bathed in the faint glow of a blue light that shone beyond the bedroom door. The clock on the nightstand read 11:20. He had been asleep for a few hours, but it seemed like only a few minutes, as if entire days should be missing from memory. He felt a strange compulsion to go to his window, pull back the curtain to make sure his suite still overlooked Manila Bay. The midnight hour. He felt as if the safehouse was about to become the most dangerous place on earth.

McBain heard many voices in the living room, peered at the glow of lights, heard the rustling of men moving about, a clack of instruments, maybe a fax machine, then heard a phone ringing.

"What the hell is going on?" McBain growled, rising.

The Russian goon tossed the trousers and a sports shirt on the bed, along with a towel. "You were having another bad dream, Comrade General. I came when I heard you cry out. I suggest you wipe yourself off."

The insolent bastard, smearing it in his face. The goon had a point, though, as McBain became aware he was soaked in sweat. Quickly he dried the moisture off his face and body, then dressed. The Russian held his arm out, and McBain headed for the living room.

The strange blue light intensified as he peered around the sprawling living room. He froze. Seven dark figures sat behind a long wooden table that wasn't there when he had gone to bed with the women. With the blue light shining behind their heads, he couldn't see their faces. But he did see at least a dozen new gunmen, all armed with automatic weapons, scattered around the living room, standing at attention, as grim as death.

The shadow in the middle of the table cleared his throat, said in a thickly accented voice, "Comrade General, I wish I could say welcome to Manila. Given all that has happened in the past few days, I am afraid I can do nothing less than tell you that at this time, the Coalition finds itself facing a crisis that could destroy us before we have a chance to enter the final phase of our operation."

McBain became even more afraid right then than he had been of the tall, dark stranger. The Coalition had sent an interrogation committee to Manila.

"Comrade General, I will ask you a very serious

question, one that will decide how I will proceed with you.''

During the long pause, McBain felt a fresh outbreak of sweat trickling down his face and neck like ice water. Forget dreams of godlike wealth and power, he decided, looking around at the grim armed men, the faceless shadows in the blue light. Suddenly just staying alive became the greatest single reward he could reap from his years of treason.

''Comrade General, have you in any way, shape or form betrayed us?''

Another round of silence became deafening, to the point where McBain heard his heart beating in his ears.

3

Mack Bolan was suffering from more than mere jet lag. It had been a long time since he felt so bone weary and frustrated—but determined. Within a few minutes adrenaline would put it in high gear for the Executioner and his Stony Man ally. Shortly the hit on the Manila warehouse would let the enemy targets know that someone was once again dogging their footsteps.

Even still, as Bolan stretched out in a prone position on the southeast edge of the warehouse rooftop, he couldn't help but feel the countless miles of continent hopping, the endless days of pursuing his adversaries, cutting them down under his guns with a lot of help from his longtime friend and Stony Man's ace pilot, Jack Grimaldi.

How many miles logged so far? How many countries had they blitzed through only to see the main enemy targets fly on, scatter and go into hiding like cockroaches fleeing the light? How many enemy dead had piled up, the enemy leaders leaving behind their wounded, who helped point the Stony Man warriors in the right direction after focused interrogation. But the enemy forged on with a rumored agenda of wholesale extermination and domination of target nations, presumably to use them as hostage countries, springboards to launch mass death and destruction against the rest of the world. The soldiers gleaned a few answers about the enemy's agenda along the way, sure, but he still had nothing he could sink his teeth into. And certainly no clear path had been laid bare to the main enemy stronghold housing the brains, money and soul behind the organization.

It had all taken a toll on Bolan, and if he was feeling it, he knew Grimaldi was also frayed. They weren't supermen, superhuman. They felt the miles, and a tired soldier could drop his guard, lose the edge, get killed.

Nearly a week had passed on the global manhunt, but it felt like a lifetime already. What had begun as some pointed questions to a former New York senator about a conspiracy between former U.S. soldiers and top Pentagon brass in collusion with ex-KGB killers, had touched off full-scale war between Bolan and the elusive enemy.

How many deadly engagements?

It had started with the ex-senator, who had died in an attack on his Long Island estate, an assault meant to silence a wagging patriotic tongue that had sent more than a few rogue intelligence agents and military brass to prison during a lengthy Senate investigation. The assassination of the ex-senator had been followed up by a suicide Muslim army that had spilled untold rivers of innocent blood in the streets of Manhattan, a foreign terrorist army imported to the States by a former U.S. Army Special Forces major gone rogue for both money and warped ideology, it appeared. From the States the mission then took Bolan to Colombia, where the enemy saw a freighter—stuffed with cocaine destined for the Russian Mafia—

blown apart by Grimaldi's F-15E to sink to the depths of the Caribbean.

The opposition worked for some shadow organization Bolan believed called itself either the Coalition or Hydra, and the enemy was on the run, at least the frontline troops were, looking for quick cash to keep their goal of Armageddon in sight or to impress their superiors. The Executioner tracked them to the south of France, rooting them out of their mountain stronghold in the Pyrenees, following on to Germany, closing shop on the enemy troops wherever he found them. Always he was faced with more, meaner and angrier and more scared than the last dead bunch.

Next came Lebanon, where an army of Shiite fanatics was set to buy a major shipment of chemical and germ weapons. That deal and more enemies had been crushed into the soil of the Bekaa Valley.

Most recently the action had taken Bolan to Pakistan, where a former Pakistani colonel turned drug lord—a long-time associate of one Petre Kuschka, former KGB killer—had bought some enriched nuclear material and component parts for a reactor, ostensibly from North Korea, to be turned around and sold to Kuschka. Once again the prime enemy targets had come up short, losing their potential nuke payload when the ship was seized by the U.S. Navy, thanks to informants inside Karachi. Whether the talking heads were CIA or the enemy's own turncoats, Bolan didn't know.

That was yesterday.

More than a full twenty-four hours had now elapsed since the Pakistani shutdown, time enough for the enemy to fly east, it appeared, to lick their wounds and reorganize. Bolan and Grimaldi had likewise regrouped, resting at the U.S. military base in Saudi Arabia. Once contact was made with Hal Brognola, both sides getting each other up to speed, the big Fed had come through for Bolan, using his clout with CIA contacts.

There had been a William McBain sighting in Manila.

Bolan counted his blessings that the hunt could resume so quickly. Figure the Philippine archipelago encompassed some 115,000 square miles, a third of it jungle, two-thirds mountainous, then factor in more than seven thousand islands, spanning almost fifteen hundred miles north to south, and the traitorous former five-star general had shown up, bold as ever, on the largest island, Luzon, and in full view of CIA agents who had Manila staked out. When Bolan and Grimaldi had touched down in the F-15E at a private airfield, two Company operatives had been on hand to greet the two men. The CIA agents were on standing orders to give Bolan and Grimaldi full cooperation, carte blanche.

The Executioner shook off the ghosts of the nightmare journey as he spotted the armed shadows in the loading bays of the warehouse.

He gave his surroundings a hard search. The warehouse district had already been reconned, and Bolan had found a suitable adjacent launch point in a warehouse shut down for the night—in with a lock pick, up onto the catwalk, through the skylight.

Togged in blacksuit, the Executioner knew he blended in with the night. A soft breeze, rife with salt, maybe carrying the stink of sweat and refuse, the eternal smell of suffering and human misery from the Tondo slums just across the Pasig River, assaulted

Bolan's senses. South he saw the walled city of In-
tramuros, the spires of churches and cathedrals rising
from that direction. The lit skyline of metro Manila
was farther inland, the occasional blaring horns, the
hubbub of Filipino throngs on the night move barely
reaching his ears. Otherwise there was very little activity around Bolan in the area around the docks and
wharves of Manila's south harbor.

The targeted warehouse was selected by Bolan as
the new starting point. Thanks to intel going to the
CIA via the native DEA troops, restless to shut down
a major heroin-trafficking operation in Manila, the
soldier knew the warehouse was a transshipment center for heroin coming in from Thailand. The owner
was one Bernaldi "Benny" Pinchinko, a Filipino
businessman. Pinchinko also owned the New Hotel
Manila where McBain was holed up. Further, the
New Hotel Manila was built by NorAmAsian, a con-
glomerate of American and Asian businessmen who
had grown big and bold with myriad business interests in Manila and points north in Hong Kong and
Singapore and beyond. According to Stony Man Farm
intel, NorAmAsian had gotten ahead with a lot of
financial aid by the World Bank Center. The pieces
of the Hydra puzzle were still jagged, but they were
coming together, piece by bloody piece. The World
Bank Center was where Kuschka, McBain and former
Special Forces Major Ben Calhoun put their millions
of illicit dollars. Bolan knew the Justice Department
was right then tearing like a cyclone through the
WBC's main branch in Germany. Its eastern branch
was in Manila.

The plan was simple enough, but Bolan was realist
enough to know anything could go wrong at any time.

If Calhoun and Kuschka were somewhere in the Philippines, then Bolan would crank up the heat, fan the flames in their direction via the nervous front men and shareholders in NorAmAsian. After what he'd seen in other countries, instinct told the soldier the men he was after were holding hands with Pinchinko and NorAmAsian. Once Bolan started the fires in the viper's nest, he was hoping either Calhoun or Kuschka or both would come slithering out. Either way, a lot of heads were due to roll in Manila. The Executioner was going to bag Pinchinko and use the man as a human shield, or bartering chip to get him inside the New Hotel Manila.

Kneeling, the Executioner threaded the customized sound suppressor on the M-16, set the assault rifle for one-shot mode. He looked through the infrared scope, adjusted the sights. He lined up the padlock on the chain-link fence. Attached to the M-16 was an M-203 grenade launcher. From the satchel, Bolan pulled out a half-dozen 40 mm grenades, a mix of fragmentation and incendiary bombs. He loaded the M-203's breech with a high-explosive round. It was something of a plus the target warehouse was built mostly of timber. Bolan figured the place would burn to the ground within minutes.

He picked up his handheld radio and patched through to Grimaldi.

The ace pilot was two blocks north in a rented sedan, armed and waiting for the word from Bolan to roll.

It was just about show time.

THEY WERE ABOUT to spring a human rat trap, Jack Grimaldi thought, only he was the cheese.

The Stony Man pilot drove up to the front gate. In the headlights of the four-door sedan, he saw the padlock, scarred by the big guy's bullet, on the ground. Beyond the gate Grimaldi counted six armed shadows on the loading dock, hustling crates from a truck. Word was the place was supposedly a storehouse for computers and computer parts. So why all the guns unless they had something more valuable to protect?

It was the same brazen display the ace pilot had seen since the global hunt had begun. Another warehouse, different city; thugs working for legitimate bosses who sidelined as major criminal conspirators. Grimaldi felt he was worlds away from when it had all begun, and he was feeling ten years older than he did a week earlier. With little sleep, near around-the-clock hunting and killing of an elusive enemy, the Stony Man pilot was almost glad to be the one-man ground strike force this time out. He was a pilot by nature, but this time he had insisted on an up-close and personal touch. Besides, the big guy was better suited as the sniper for this outing, hitting them from above while Grimaldi threw it in their face, point-blank.

Stepping out of the sedan, Grimaldi walked to the gate and pushed it open. He heard a startled voice in the distance shout, "Hey!"

Grimaldi hopped back in the car. Blood racing, heart pounding, he fisted the mini-Uzi, which was cocked and locked. The plan was risky, but it seemed it was all they had to go with—hit the various businesses of Bernaldi Pinchinko, burn them down, hopefully bag a mouthpiece who would relay a grim message to Manila's front man for NorAmAsian. McBain would circle the wagons, flush out Calhoun and

Kuschka and if the prize targets were gathered in Manila, the Stony Man warriors could bait them out of hiding. If that didn't work, they would find a way to penetrate the top floor of the New Hotel Manila and bag a renegade Pentagon five-star general.

The ace pilot was through the gate as three slightly built, long-haired Filipinos with subguns slung across their shoulders moved from the bay. Halfway across the lot Grimaldi stopped as they continued their beeline for the sedan.

He knew the big guy was perched on the warehouse rooftop directly behind. Bolan was an expert marksman. His silenced M-16 had an effective range of 400 meters. The Executioner was no more than a quarter of that distance to the west. Chip shot. The attached M-203 could hit a target accurately up to 350 meters. The targets were either human, lined up along the bay, or the scattered five windows along the west face of the warehouse.

Grimaldi put on an innocent smile. "How you guys doing tonight?"

"You are trespassing on private property," the middle hardman growled. "What do you want?"

Beyond the trio, Grimaldi spotted two more gunmen, obviously suspecting something was wrong, step out into the open.

"I want to deliver a message. Starting with you three," Grimaldi said, his voice going hard. "Pinchinko's going out of the heroin business."

Their expressions changed right away from ill-concealed paranoia to lethal intent, and they made their move. He waited until they began sliding the SMGs off their shoulders, then Grimaldi started to shut the trap. It was a tough shot, snapping up the mini-Uzi, shooting across his body out the window. But Grimaldi got the job done just the same, holding back on the trigger, stitching them with a line of 9 mm slugs, left to right. Before his blaze of lead tore into the third hardman, who nearly had him lined up with the SMG, Grimaldi saw the side of the guy's head explode.

Grimaldi gunned the engine, watching as Bolan drilled a well-placed round into a hardman's leg downrange. The other shadow pitched to the ground a heartbeat later, twitched once, then went utterly still.

The night then erupted in fire and thunder.

The first explosion took out a cluster of armed men along the loading bay, stick figures flung in all directions, shredded by angry flames and superheated shrapnel. Next the windows began to absorb the Executioner's potent mix of HE and incendiary rounds. Grimaldi left Bolan to it as he raced up on the wounded man. Just as the hardman, clutching his leg, reached for his discarded subgun, Grimaldi thrust open the door and laid the guy out with a metallic headache. Stepping out, the ace pilot scanned the smoking bay, found no one moving. The side of the warehouse erupted on in ear-shattering detonations.

Grimaldi pinned his prisoner with a steely look. "You speak English?"

The Filipino gritted his teeth, nodded. "Who are you?"

"A major headache for your boss. Tell Pinchinko the five-star general, the major and the Russians are not welcome in Manila. Repeat that for me."

The hardman did and Grimaldi hopped into the sedan. He rolled back toward the gate to pick up Bolan. They had a shopping list, and this was merely the first

stop. It was going to be a long and tough night for
the bad guys in Manila.

The glowing band of fire flickered in Grimaldi's
rearview. It was hot as hell, even at that hour, but the
two Stony Man warriors had only begun to turn up
the heat.

4

Before he could answer the life-or-death question, the cellular phone beeped. McBain hated himself for flinching at the sudden noise, then forced himself to stand rigidly at attention before the shadows. Try as he might to put on a brave face, he grew more afraid with each passing second under their cold and silent scrutiny. He wished he could see their faces, at least, but that damnable blue light was some unearthly shroud, blinding him to their identities.

As if it mattered.

His life was hanging in the balance; of course someone had to play the scapegoat. It looked as if he had been chosen for the part.

A few more beeps, and finally the middle shadow at the table answered the phone, conducting his side of the conversation in both Russian and English. McBain listened, if nothing else, aware he had a momentary reprieve.

And just who was he supposed to have betrayed? Kuschka? Calhoun? The Coalition hierarchy? How? Why? He had just as much to lose as anyone involved, behind or on the front lines. By God, he had invested his own money in the Coalition, working the drug and arms deals right there with Calhoun and others in the CIA, growing filthy rich in the process, but sweating nonetheless over the years at being found a traitor, terrified of being marched up before self-righteous, indignant politicians like many of his former pals, tried, convicted and locked up for life. Why would he just turn around now and piss on their feet?

"*Da...da...da.* I see. *Ponimayo.* Understood. I am glad you are safe."

McBain could feel their stares, boring into him from behind the blue cloak. He felt the sweat break out on his forehead. He wanted a smoke, needed a drink. He gave his surroundings another search, feeling more like some hot virus under a microscope than part of the human race, much less on the same team as the shadows. A computer bank was set up in the far corner of the suite, and black-clad figures, backs to him, were hunched over terminals. The gunmen seemed to multiply around him with the second look. About twenty-plus goons occupied the suite, holding AKs. In just a few short hours, the suite had been turned into a command center—or a fortress. Obviously word of their nightmarish woes had reached the upper echelons of the Coalition, and the shadows had been sent scurrying to circle the wagons. Kill or be killed, no doubt. Maybe the killing would start with one former Pentagon counterintelligence five-star general who had outlived his usefulness.

McBain caught some of the Russian. He heard *pjos* and CIA *kalorshniks.* "Dogs" and "criminals." He heard a short, angry one-sided exchange, picked up Russian curse words. He heard about their comrades in Moscow who were most unhappy. The Russian Mafia. Still more human sharks circling somewhere, ready to pounce, still more hard feelings that someone on the home team wasn't playing it straight. But a billion dollars' worth of ninety percent cocaine was nothing to just shrug off. Cutting the Russian Mafia in for a piece of the action to fatten their own bank accounts had proved another serious complication. McBain had to wonder what Kuschka had promised his comrades in the Russian Mafia, how many lies had been told to them. And if Kuschka was out there, jerking his own people around...

"Yes, he is here and he is safe."

Kuschka was on the other end, McBain thought, and felt his spine tighten with fear. What was Kuschka saying about him? Getting the shadow up to speed, no doubt, detailing the series of fiascos that had nearly destroyed them all. Passing the buck? Incriminating him?

"I understand. It is all most unfortunate. It is why I am here, to clean up the messes you and your men have unfortunately left behind while you make your way home. Understood. I understand. I will know more shortly. I will contact you in precisely one hour with further instructions."

Abruptly the shadow ended the communication, removed something from the cellular phone and checked it—probably a scrambling device, McBain thought—then set the phone on the table. The silence became total, deafening.

"Well, Comrade General? I am waiting."

McBain cleared his throat, dredged up all the courage he could command. "You're asking me, I assume, if I have something to do with or have some knowledge about the series of disasters and setbacks myself and the others have suffered."

"You assume correct."

"No, I have nothing to do with what's happened to us. That's all I can tell you."

"Really?"

"I have just as much to lose as anybody else involved."

"Is that a fact?"

"I have been an aid and an ally to the KGB for thirty-some years. What I have done for them is known to them, and I have proved myself an invaluable asset."

"Is that so?"

A large black duffel bag appeared on the table, and the middle shadow slid it away from the blue light.

"Do you recognize that, Comrade General?"

McBain swallowed hard. The bastards had found his stash. "I recognize it."

"Quite the nest egg."

"Funds for a rainy day."

"Indeed. Perhaps it is raining a little too hard?"

"I wasn't planning on abandoning ship, if that's what you're implying."

"Is that a fact?"

"Yes, that's a fact."

"Even if the ship appears to be sinking?"

"I haven't given up hope."

"That is very good to hear. It brings me to the next matter. As of this afternoon, your accounts in the World Bank Center have been cleaned out. We are now in possession of your money."

McBain heard the roar of fury in his ears. He was mentally tabbing their pilfering, figured it was somewhere in the neighborhood of twenty-five to thirty million dollars, U.S. Factor in investments, stocks, bonds...

"I earned that money."

"Indeed. However, there is more at stake here, Comrade General, than your mere accumulation of wealth. Wealth, need I remind you, that came from our hand that fed you all these years. Provided you with whores, and fancy homes around the world. Provided you with protection from discovery."

"Who the hell are you people, anyway? Why don't you ask what you want to know and stop jerking my chain?"

Silence, then the shadow said, "Who I am is of no importance to you. What I am is, shall I say, your counterpart in the intelligence-military community. First, you work for the Coalition—your money and your contacts, whether you are aware of it, have helped mount and finance the Hydra Project. That money you are so worried about technically belongs to us. Suffice it to say, I am formerly of the VGK, the Soviet Supreme High Command. I am Kuschka's immediate superior. We have never met each other, Comrade General, but I know everything about you. For instance, I know how we used women—'swallows,' I believe they are called in your intelligence circle—in Western Europe, in your own country, in Colombia so long ago. So many cocktails, so much laughter, so many hotel suites, nights of passion and promise. Ah, but to be young and virile again, no? Do you remember Ilyanka? Natasha?" A chuckle. "We still have pictures, video, taped conversations among other evidence, your weakness for the flesh of women other than your wife, may she rest in peace. However, blackmail is not what we will resort to at this time."

He winced, felt a momentary stab of anger, resentment, even self-hate. It was all something McBain had long since wanted to forget. In the beginning there had been the pictures, taken of him with young Russian women, KGB plants. There had been blackmail, then some bartering on his part with the KGB, aware his whole life could go up in smoke, divorce, disgrace, court-martial, the whole ugly nine yards. Better to play ball with the KGB, take their money and run, feed them counterintelligence when they demanded it.

That was thirty-odd years ago, during what he saw as the dirty beginning of America's decline. The sixties. The hippies, the draft dodgers, all the rights movements, the screaming and whining that eventually drowned out the voices of reason and distorted morality and basic human decency, when he was back then fighting a war that should have been winnable from the onset, but was turned into a ten-thousand-day debacle by men in government, the military hierarchy and the intelligence community who profited off the suffering and dying of the basic grunt. It was all a sham, a game where the only winner was the one who had the most money, the most assets. It had become a material world, after all, and he was going to jump aboard the gravy train before it left the station.

Back then he had read the proverbial writing on the wall, decided to lead the charge of the cynical realists before he took it in the shorts because he still believed in democracy and justice for all. Screw that. The whole country, hell, the whole world was changing, and for the worse. Hell, the list of social ills was endless, and it was hopeless to attempt to stand up and take on the foamy-mouth hordes of unreason unless you had a weapon of mass destruction to threaten them with, hold them back.

So much for salvation, hope, a brighter tomorrow. The only reason he ever bought into the Coalition's program of nuclear, bio and chem blackmail was that he'd been promised his own safe haven, a fat source of money and all the pleasure he could taste. The commoners, of course, the civilians, the handwringers and bleeding hearts, he thought, might see that as shallow, cruel, selfish, whatever, but he didn't give a damn about what they thought. In a way he hoped the Coalition pulled off its crazy agenda. There were a lot of wrongs that needed righting, and whatever he used to believe was the backbone of America—life, liberty and the pursuit of happiness—only existed at the barrel of a gun or a whopping bank account.

It occurred to him right then he no longer had either. The shadow's cold, gravelly voice jerked McBain back to the moment of truth.

"Yes, I see you are perhaps remembering your humble origins. From what I have gathered from my own sources, I know you know something of what we are all about. Let me bring you up-to-date on whatever you think you know, whatever briefings you received in your dealings with Kuschka. We are about reshaping a world gone mad. We are about changing everything on the face of this planet, from who owns what, to the very system of money, international trading and so on.

"A select few have been chosen to lead the way. We have the best of Russian brains and muscle behind us. Among the chosen elsewhere are military men, intelligence agents, even, to my distaste, major international criminals on the run who want refuge and guaranteed twilight years of peace and pleasure and dominion over their empires. This plan of global domination has been in the works for nearly three decades. There are deposed dictators and former heads of state who share our views, who have been paid some of what was promised them in U.S. dollars in order for us to return them to power and for them to allow us to work with them in reshaping their countries. These countries stretch around the world—Asia, Africa, Eastern Europe, South America, one small but obscenely oil-rich country in the Middle East. We have the money, the matériel, the means, the manpower. We have acquired the brains of doomsday, and we have developed advanced weapons of mass destruction never before known to man. One item. And believe what you will, it matters not. We have agents about to be unknowingly infected with a hot virus, a level-four virus, that would make Ebola Zaire look like the common cold—only we have the antiviral cure. It is only one method we will use to subjugate and conquer those who need to be retrained in our way of thinking.''

''I don't know that I have much stomach for Armageddon at my age, Comrade General, or whoever you are.''

''But, of course. You came aboard to save yourself, to get what you could from us. Understandable if not forgivable. You misjudge perhaps. We are about saving the human race, not destroying it. When you signed on as eyes and ears for the KGB then the drug cartels, you sold your soul to us, if you believe in such a thing as a soul. I understand you were promised a country of your choosing once a new world order is established? At this stage, given our current crisis, all promises are on hold.''

"So, I'm a prisoner here, maybe on death row in my own suite until you see how things are going to fall.''

The shadow said nothing for several moments, then answered, "It would seem two men have been hunting you, the major and Kuschka across several continents. These troubles all began in your country. These men are faceless, nameless, but they appear hell-bent on your destruction. And if they wish to destroy you...well, I was somewhat opposed to the attack in New York from the beginning. But I allowed the major to proceed, through Kuschka, wondering if such an attack would either show us the extent of our American comrades' loyalty or ferret out unforeseen problems. Unfortunately since Manhattan our entire agenda is threatened. Incredibly, with all our vast resources, I am unable to determine the identity of our enemies, and they are 'our' enemies. Or are they?''

"Again, you suspect I know something," McBain said. "I've been privy to a lot of black operations over the years, but this is something that goes way beyond anything my government would sanction. We have been tracked, attacked and nearly annihilated and repeatedly. No matter where we go, they seem to show up. They have access to information, intelligence about us and, worse, access to some serious heavy firepower, including fighter jets and state-of-the-art helicopter gunships.''

"I understand you had a face-to-face with one of these men in France?''

McBain recalled his ominous meeting in the French village with the tall stranger. Kuschka had been on hand during what was in McBain's mind a test of wills before the sky once again dropped on them.

"Yes," McBain answered. "But you already know that from Kuschka. I have never seen the man before."

McBain waited while the shadow conversed in low tones with another shadow.

"At this time, Comrade General, I will accept everything for what it appears. A most disturbing mystery. But a crisis nonetheless. Understand that we have many contacts, business ventures here in the Philippines, but perhaps you already know of our backers in Manila."

"That would be NorAmAsian."

"Precisely. We have helped each other grow rich in the East. The money has greatly helped the Coalition. I would hate to cause our people here in Manila any of the sort of problems that might have followed you to Manila."

"Sounds like a threat."

"Simply voicing my concern."

"You're thinking we could have trouble here in Manila and if that happens, then you'll keep looking my way."

"So far, there has been no sign of the kind of trouble in Manila that you have had in other countries. Other than, of course, the ever present lurking nuisance of the CIA. In fact they have this hotel under surveillance."

Great, McBain bitterly thought. And now the Company knew a Russian goon squad, armed to the teeth, had pulled up the drawbridge in his suite.

"If you have been honest with us, Comrade General, then you have nothing to fear. Once Kuschka and the major arrive, we will all be once again one big happy family. The losses of men and matériel are recoverable. However, should your problems in the form of two unknown enemies show up in Manila...well a bloodbath in this hotel and the city streets would make my associates in NorAmAsian very nervous and unhappy.''

"You never answered my original question."

"Very well. You are confined to the suite. We will provide you with everything you need."

McBain peered into the blue light, resisting the urge to reach out and grab someone by the throat. They owned his money, his life, his balls. He was on board to the bitter end. Everything he needed, he angrily thought. Did that include the bullet for his own execution?

THE GUY WAS JUST a pimp to the local authorities, who were most likely bought and paid for by his money and favors. How else could the man stay in business for so long, with a criminal record behind him, including arrest for distribution of narcotics, which was supposedly punishable by death in the Philippines? Corruption then was big business in Manila, like in many other poor countries where the only way certain men believed they could get ahead in an ugly world meant to keep them down—grab the good life through the shortcut of crime—was to prey on the blood, the misery and the weaknesses of their fellow man, thus only making it all a little uglier.

If the climb to the top of the heap for Pando Coura had been ugly, then Mack Bolan intended the fall to be downright hideous. In the Executioner's bigger scheme of things, he would use Pando Coura as a human pawn to both relay a grim message to Pinchinko and hopefully shake the viper's nest some more, while likewise maneuvering the main targets into place on Bolan's chessboard of death.

Not to mention, of course, the Executioner had come to burn down Coura's house, set free whatever innocents he found inside the man's den of human suffering.

According to CIA and DEA intelligence, backed up by Stony Man Farm which had put together Bolan's Manila hit list, Coura was a major mover and shaker in prostitution, narcotics and the export of young Filipina girls, most of whom were drugged or hauled by force from their villages or had their parents' silence and cooperation bought or coerced by the end of a gun. Some of the girls went willingly, of course, but there were reports many went against their will after repeated rape and forced drug use.

Indeed, there were plenty of poisonous snakes to be stepped on in Manila.

Coura had of late put on a legitimate face, becoming an associate and shareholder in the "nightclub" business in Manila with Pinchinko. What Bolan was concerned about, was the word of a DEA informant who knew Coura sat on, refined and moved huge amounts of heroin, allegedly from a secret basement lab. And at any given time, at least three or four dozen Filipina girls were confined to squalid quarters, used and abused, or waiting for the right shining knight to come along with ready cash.

Bolan braced himself to find anything, ready for the worst when he entered Coura's abode. He looked down the dark, narrow avenue, feeling the heat of the Manila midnight hour. Half a block away, Grimaldi remained in the sedan, backup on this hit, ready to come through the front door when the Executioner needed assistance. The miniature one-way radio bug in Bolan's pants pocket would keep his one-man backup informed of when to make his move.

The soldier strolled up to the open, manicured lawn of the large building. Recon, ten minutes earlier, had shown the structure to be made of timber.

That would work.

Beneath his loose-fitting windbreaker, Bolan toted the .44 Magnum Desert Eagle on his hip, the Beretta 93-R snugged in shoulder holster. In the pockets of his jacket he carried one fragmentation grenade, two incendiary bombs, specifically meant to create a firestorm that would be seen for miles away. There was a different touch this time around, something businesslike, unsuspecting, or so he hoped. With the black briefcase in hand, Bolan walked up to the steel door and gave the night one last search. Fatigue made him wonder if the enemy would always be one step ahead.

They were just a few blocks north of the Tondo slums. The targeted building sat in a run-down residential area of dark hovels that somehow looked obscene on the palm-tree-lined streets. The area was crawling with shadows of hookers, soldiers, Filipinos who caroused the intersecting street that was lined with bars and strip joints. There was enough racket on the street, enough seedy activity to hopefully buy Bolan and Grimaldi some time to leave the scene once their goal was furthered.

Moving on might prove the easiest part.

Bolan had no idea the enemy numbers, or how many innocent young women would be confined in the building. He would take the action as it showed, burn them down where they rose to fight. If Pinchinko was taking a fat slice of Coura's action in the flesh-narco trade, then toppling the enemy here could prove a major coup for Bolan.

The soldier rapped on the steel door, waited. A slat opened, and suspicious dark eyes peered back at the Executioner.

Bolan put on his best anxious face, the look of a lost and bewildered Yankee. "Uh, hello, my name is Samuel Tomlin. I was sent here by a friend of a friend of Mr. Pinchinko. I was told of a mutual business interest I could find here if I were to speak with one Mr. Coura."

"There's no one here by that name. Go away now."

Bolan held up the briefcase. "I was quoted a price by this associate of Mr. Pinchinko. Since I'm short on time and have to leave Manila in the morning, I figured I would double the asking price in order to expedite matters."

Dark eyes narrowed the gaze, the wheels spinning. No matter what, money talked, and it surely opened doors.

The slat closed, dead bolts and other locks rattled and clicked. A huge, swarthy Filipino with a holstered .45 Colt filled the doorway. With the paranoia that came naturally to criminals, the giant looked past Bolan, searching the street both ways. His gaze then settled on the briefcase.

"Inside."

The Executioner brushed past the man. As he stepped into a narrow hallway, Bolan saw two more armed hardmen move through a beaded archway, dead ahead.

The steel door shut with a thudding finality behind Bolan.

"The money first, then you see Mr. Coura."

Bolan made a show of looking nervously at the Uzi submachine guns slung across the shoulders of the two Filipinos at the end of the short hall. Mentally the Executioner was already mapping out his attack strategy. The metallic thumping of rock and roll sounded from somewhere on the second story.

Bolan nodded, said, "Why, of course."

Even as the giant took the briefcase and flipped the latches open, Bolan dropped his hand by his side, ready to make his move for the Desert Eagle.

The giant opened an empty briefcase. Instead of reacting with surprise or outrage, the giant paused, then hurled the briefcase at Bolan's head.

5

Bolan deflected the briefcase with an arm. In the same motion he dug out the .44 Magnum Desert Eagle and went to gruesome work in the following heartbeat.

The three Filipino hardmen were making their play, hell-bent on taking it to the limit, no hesitating, no stops in between after they realized they had been duped by their own greed to let in an unknown factor. Even as they began to bring their weapons to bear, Bolan read the flicker of uncertainty and fear in their eyes. No doubt they were wondering for that critical split second before opening fire who the hell he was—narc, Fed, maybe a ticked-off customer who had come down with AIDS thanks to one of their more seriously damaged goods.

None of the above, but they would never know that.

Mack Bolan was the Executioner, and he had come to steamroller Pando Coura and flunkies before moving on to the next game in town.

The Desert Eagle roared in Bolan's hand. The first slug tore into the giant Filipino, just below the sternum. Shot at point-blank range, Bolan's first victim was lifted off his feet, a look of dumbfounded agony making his eyes bulge like some gargoyle mask as he was flung into the wall.

As luck had it, the briefcase, after bouncing off Bolan's arm, continued to sail down the hall, twirling straight for the face of one of the Uzi subgunners, altering that Filipino's aim, making him dance out of the path of the leather missile.

Crouched and pivoting, Bolan caressed the big stainless-steel hand cannon's trigger, blowing the dancer off his feet with the second .44 round.

The third subgunner held his ground, the muzzle of his Uzi unleashing a brief spray of 9 mm lead. Bolan caught the giant coming his way, dead on his feet, after rebounding off the wall, which ran slick with his spattered blood. The human mountain next shielded Bolan from the tracking rounds of 9 mm Parabellum manglers, as the giant took the lead projectiles up the side. Shredded flesh and blood flew past the soldier, who was already tracking his next target, aiming low around his human shield.

The Desert Eagle thundered again, but the Filipino subgunner darted to one side, seeing the sudden twist of events that might leave him fully exposed to the tall invader.

Even still Bolan scored a leg hit. The man's scream shattered the air as the .44 slug punched the leg out from under him, sent him crumpling to the floor. The guy curled up in a fetal position, clutching his leg, moaning.

On the move, Bolan took in his surroundings, rapidly reviewing what little he knew about the drug-prostitution fortress.

At the end of the hall, around the corner, a set of wooden steps led to a second story. Up there, in separate rooms, the human merchandise was stored and guarded, reportedly, by a handful of Filipino thugs.

Beyond the beaded curtain, ahead of Bolan, was supposedly Coura's "love nest." According to the information gathered by the CIA, the room doubled as a porn set and pleasure den for the pimp. Shouts and shrill female screams from beyond the curtain revealed to Bolan the intel was proving accurate. The rough guess of gunmen in the place was tagged at around a dozen, give or take. Long odds, again, but Bolan had beaten back worse odds before.

Even still, he was rolling the dice, fully aware he could come up snake eyes anytime.

"Blow the door down!" Bolan said, knowing Grimaldi was already en route, but alerting his ally to the fact that he was clear of the coming blast.

Up top doors were opening, and at least four hardmen scrambled into Bolan's view, their subguns poised to fire, a couple of them in different states of undress, sweaty from exerting their own brand of warm-up on girls about to be peddled out of the country. They were shouting in their native tongue, minds trying to piece together the action, their expressions anxious, confused.

Bolan snapped up a discarded Uzi, hit a crouch just beside the beaded archway and gave them even more reason to shout. The Executioner held back on the trigger of the subgun, raking the upstairs, right to left. Several wild rounds from chattering subguns searched Bolan out but drilled into the floor beside him, whining off stone, slapping into the wall. Without missing a beat, the Executioner nailed the four hardmen in a neat line of sweeping 9 mm slugs. Under his steady barrage of Uzi lead, they toppled, human bowling pins.

"Make sure my back's covered from the front hall,

then check the upstairs and get the women rounded up,'' Bolan said, giving silent thanks to Gadgets Schwarz, Stony Man's electronics wizard, for supplying him with the supersensitive bug, a device that didn't require a throat mike or handheld radio to relay his words.

Bolan saw the Filipino he had wounded make a grandstand play. The knife was out of its ankle sheath and flashing for the Executioner's face. Because of the guy's wound he couldn't put enough snap behind the swipe. Bolan dodged the blade easily, then grabbed his adversary by the shoulder and hurled him through the archway. The guy had gone for broke, and a second later Bolan discovered just how badly the knifeman had crapped out.

Autofire rang out from beyond the curtain. Bolan followed the Filipino inside, hit the floor and rolled up behind a divan. Beside the Executioner the Filipino was jerking around as his comrades nailed him in a blind panic. The force of the bullets tearing into him seemed to hold him upright despite a useless leg. The guy took a face of angry betrayal as his death mask before he finally crumpled in a boneless sprawl.

The soldier popped up, took in the commotion.

He had barged into a mini-Hollywood studio in Manila. At least four naked Filipinas were scurrying from a giant waterbed, screaming and bowling down cameras and lights.

The Uzi stammered to action in Bolan's fists, tracking for the only three armed men he found in the studio. Their subguns rattled on even as they took Bolan's lead, the gunmen too late in adjusting their aim to the new and the only threat in the room. Their wild rounds shattered cameras, erupting glass and

sparks, as they spun and pitched backward, doing
their own version of a stage exit.

Bolan scanned on. A small, swarthy figure with
long black hair did an awkward tumble off the satin
sheets of the bed. He grabbed up a robe, but that
couldn't conceal the face Bolan had already branded
into memory from a previous intel photo.

It looked as if Pando Coura was tired of being an
unknown celebrity.

Beyond the archway the soldier heard the brief stutter of weapons fire as he rolled for Coura. Grimaldi
was hard at work, he hoped, and Bolan sent his friend
silent blessings that he made quick and easy work of
whatever enemy numbers were left upstairs.

Coura's black mane fell across his face as he struggled into a purple satin robe.

As he advanced on the pimp, Bolan kept an eye on
his surroundings, checked his flanks. Other than a few
scattered beds, chairs, couches, a love seat, and man-
acles and whips, among other sexual paraphernalia,
all props for Coura's overseas porn market, there was
little of value in the studio. Floor-to-ceiling curtains
covered the windows. They looked suitable enough
to suck up angry flames and help bring down the
house of Coura within minutes flat for what the soldier had in mind. Only Bolan needed the premises
cleared of all innocents. He knew Grimaldi was busy
rounding up the girls right then.

"Stay put," Bolan told the young women, their
eyes burning with terror as they shrugged into robes.

Suddenly a figure appeared in the corner of Bolan's
eye. The gunman rose, as if by magic, from a hole in
the floor. He was bringing a subgun into view when
the side of his head erupted in blood and gore. Bolan

looked over his shoulder at Grimaldi, who was standing in the archway, a wisp of smoke coming from the muzzle of his Uzi.

"Check the upstairs?"

"They're coming down now. We look clear at least from where I'm standing. A few johns, but I sent them packing."

"Round up the women in the hall," Bolan told his friend. "One minute and counting before we put the torch to this place."

"What do you want? Who the fuck are you?"

Bolan turned an icy stare on Coura. "I'm a PR man for safe sex. I'll ask the questions."

In response to the pimp's curse, Bolan drew the Desert Eagle and blew out a light beside the man. Sparks and glass rained on the pimp. Coura cried out and covered his head.

"How much dope do you have downstairs?"

Coura hesitated, then chuckled, his eyes betraying to Bolan that he thought he understood what the hit was all about. "Enough. You want some, I have five hundred pounds of nearly pure heroin. I can spare a little."

Bolan played along. "You have money in here?"

"I see we can bargain. Okay. I have some in a wall safe."

"Get it."

The soldier listened to the commotion out in the hall. So far, there was no more gunfire. This was the part of town that wasn't on any Manila tour guide. If there were any local authorities close at hand, they were probably busy indulging themselves in any number of vice havens in the area. Even still, clearing the block could prove a close shave if the police showed up.

Bolan closely watched the pimp lift an oil print of a naked Asian woman off the wall, then dial the combination to the safe.

"You pull out something other than money, you'll never be able to star in one of your porn flicks again—unless you're playing a eunuch."

Coura showed Bolan the rubber-banded stacks of cash. "Fifty thousand, American."

Bolan nodded at one of the cowering women. "Give it to her."

Outraged, Coura snarled, "What? What is this game? You want me to give these whores my hard-earned money?"

"Call it a donation. You're turning over a new leaf." Bolan drew a bead on Coura's groin, the Desert Eagle rock steady in his fist. "You've got two seconds to do it."

Coura grumbled an oath, then tossed the money to a girl who Bolan figured was no more than sixteen.

"Beat it, girls," Bolan told them. They hesitated, the girl looking at the money as if it were a poisonous snake. "Take the money, leave the building." She took the money, then they stood, gathered as a group before Bolan. One of them spit on Coura and cursed him in her native tongue.

"Do you know what he does to us?" the spitter growled.

"I think I've got some idea. I want you and the others to go back to your villages, your parents, whoever, wherever you came from. Pando's going out of business."

As they began to file out, the soldier asked Coura, "How many girls you have in the building?"

"Thirty-six."

As if on cue, Grimaldi reappeared in the archway. He asked the Stony Man pilot for a head count of the women, a part of the plan they had previously outlined. Snuffing out innocent lives never fit into Bolan's combat scenario. Thirty-two, he was told. When Grimaldi asked the girls if anyone had been left behind or was hiding still upstairs, Bolan heard several anxious voices say no. If nothing else, at least thirty-six young lives would have a second chance.

"Show them out," Bolan told Grimaldi, then hauled Coura toward the trapdoor. He stood beside the hole in the floor, listening for movement below. Thinking ahead to how much clearance he might have when he touched off the firestorm, he asked, "Are there chemicals down there?"

"No. Just the merchandise, nonflammable cutting material, used to step on the merchandise. This place is made mostly of timber. The smallest of fires would raze the place within minutes."

"How about—"

As if in answer to his next question about gunmen below, a barrage of autofire chewed the trapdoor around Bolan's feet. He leaped back, hauling Coura with him as bullets kept on blazing out of the hole. The Executioner didn't have time to trade shots, ask them to come out with their hands up. Down below there were no innocents. He primed an incendiary grenade. Autofire roared on, interspersed with cursing and shouting.

Bolan pitched the grenade into the hole, grabbed Coura and hurried him toward the archway. Five seconds and counting. They hit the hallway where Grimaldi was ushering out the last of the girls, when a muffled explosion sounded in the studio, followed by the wail of men being eaten live by the lethal potion of white phosphorous.

The soldier gave Grimaldi the nod to finish the job they had started, and both men armed an incendiary grenade. Coura looked on, viciously cursing the two warriors. Grimaldi lobbed his steel egg into the upstairs hallway while Bolan pitched his grenade through the beaded archway, the stench of burning flesh piercing his senses, the bansheelike shrieking of men torched alive fading. Before moving on, Bolan glimpsed the crater in the middle of the studio's floor. Above the glimmering sheen of fire, it was raining white powder.

"You bastards! You'll pay for this! I'll hunt you down—"

Bolan snatched Coura outside, pulling the man over the steel door Grimaldi had blown down. They hit the street where the women were running down the block, in the opposite direction of their rental car. Two more explosions rocked the building.

The Executioner slid the Desert Eagle into its hip holster. "Tell Pinchinko a friend of the general in the New Hotel Manila said hello."

Coura gritted his teeth, his eyes full of savage hate. "Oh, I'll be sure to tell him, and you won't live another hour in Manila!"

The soldier snatched the robe off the pimp. "That's just to make sure you move a little faster to relay the message."

Bolan and Grimaldi beat a hasty exit for their getaway vehicle, leaving Pando Coura, naked and alone and viciously cursing the night as fire ate up his twisted ambitions.

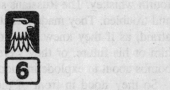

6

The Russians arrived at the same time, same day, every other week, like clockwork, and always in pairs. They were tall, dressed in black, with shaved skulls. They were also armed with ugly machine pistols that hung in holsters from their shoulders, their suit jackets opened just enough to display their weapons to Renaldo Salizar. They made him extremely nervous, but he had his orders from the director himself.

Nerves aside, his was not to reason why or question the business transaction that Mr. Pinchinko had honored him with, or so he chose to believe it was an honor. As junior vice president of NorAmAsian's TeleCom Center, with a fledgling affiliate sister company in Moscow, he was to just hand over the four briefcases stuffed with cash—U.S. dollars, of course, since rubles were still worthless despite the alleged economic boom of the new Russia.

So on this same day every two weeks, at precisely one in the morning, Salizar waited in his office. Sometimes he would count the money personally before they arrived to avoid any complaints, or sometimes he would just stare at the mahogany walls, maybe twiddle his thumbs behind his massive teak desk. Or he would go straight to the wet bar and start to make the first of two stiff whiskeys.

This night he found himself already working on his fourth whiskey. The Russians seemed especially grim and troubled. They made Renaldo Salizar particularly afraid, as if they knew some demented secret about him or his future, or they were perhaps human time bombs about to explode in sudden senseless violence.

So they stood in front of the desk, counting their take, somber, even seeming suspicious they might get shortchanged their piece of the action. It was "excess cash flow," Salizar knew, funneled through one of several dummy offshore companies or shell companies set up in Singapore and Taiwan. The cash came from what Salizar knew was the other business that went on behind the legitimate front of computers, electronics, telecommunications and so on.

He preferred to see no evil, but lately the other business was booming and the briefcases of cash were multiplying biweekly. There was a huge demand, it seemed, for pornography and narcotics in the new Russia. It was distasteful to him to have to deal with common thugs, even dangerous ones, since he was the man on the front lines handing them the "cooperation" money. But what could a man do when he hoped to be crowned successor someday to the director? He followed orders from the higher-ups, naturally, turned a blind eye to something that was outrageously profitable, after all, but would never show up in the annual reports.

Renaldo Salizar was a young up-and-coming executive in the new NorAmAsian empire. He had a cush life, built on a seven-figure salary, plus bonuses and incentives. He had his own suite on the tenth floor of the main NorAmAsian office. He had a wife and two children and, of course, the obligatory mistress.

His window overlooked Ayala Avenue, the main drag of Makati. Makati was the beating business heart of Manila, coined as the Wall Street of the Philippines. Beyond his office were streets that Salizar had walked as a boy, dreaming that someday he would be more than just a poor fisherman's son. The boy had lived long enough to fulfill the dream as a man. He was rich beyond his wildest expectations, had honor and respect. Only he had to wonder, during moments of whiskey-induced guilt, if his dead parents, devout Catholics all of their lives, would approve of his moonlighting as a coconspirator in a burgeoning international criminal organization that might some day soon make the South American drug cartels look nickel-and-dime.

Whatever, he had nearly reached the pinnacle of the NorAmAsian kingdom, and he chose to see himself as a king merely meeting the needs of his subjects, those peasant masses who needed a little excitement to get through the drudgery of their daily routine. If they were exporting sins of the flesh, then there was a demand for what they sold in the shadows, so who could blame them for simply meeting market demands?

It was a big world, and it was changing every day. A man had to keep ahead of the trends if he was going to succeed in business.

Working on his drink, Salizar left the Russians to their counting and their grunting. From where he sat he could see the Makati skyline, the strings of posh modern international hotels and four-star restaurants up and down the avenue, many of which were soon to be bought out by NorAmAsian, along with their Russian partners. He looked out at his world of lights and steel and glass, the rich young executive, the new breed of warrior, wielding fax sheets and computer chips instead of a sword or a gun. He thought about his mistress; maybe he'd stop by for a quickie at the condo he had bought for her.

Life was sweet for Renaldo Salizar.

He was watching the Russians put the bills through a computerized money counter, impatient with them to get on with it, when the phone rang. The Russians looked suspiciously at Salizar. Other than security, there was no one in the building at that hour, and no one but Mr. Pinchinko—maybe his wife or mistress— should be calling at that hour.

Salizar answered on the fourth ring. His voice guarded, he said, "Yes?"

The voice on the other end sounded as cold as ice, a graveyard voice that made Salizar's sphincter tighten as he heard, "You're going to have some trouble."

"What? What trouble? Who is this?"

Salizar was rising from his wing-back chair, visions of some major international law-enforcement squad bursting into the office branding itself in his mind. The Russians stopped counting the money, one of them even reaching for his weapon, like an animal whose survival instincts were kicking in, when the world exploded right in front of the junior vice president.

Rather, the head of the Russian in front of Salizar erupted, as if a grenade had gone off inside his bald skull. Horrified, the young executive was rooted for what felt like an eternity, as he watched the Russian, half of his head missing, crumple to the carpet, blood and muck spattering the face of his comrade who now had the machine pistol out, searching for only God knew what.

It occurred to Salizar that a sniper was firing at his office from across the street, from atop one of the hotels. He realized that was the only logical, terrifying conclusion, as he found the window of his suite had been shattered and a bed of glass shards had been blown across the office.

The Russian was shouting something in his native tongue, still searching for the invisible shooter when Salizar witnessed the second execution. Another silenced bullet drilled, dead center, through the man's chest, lifting him off his feet and hurling him back as if he were no more than a piece of paper blown in a strong wind.

Reacting, Salizar hit the floor, fearfully aware he was next.

He waited, listening to the wind howl through the obliterated opening. The next bullet never came.

"Salizar? Salizar, pick up the phone."

The graveyard voice. The phone dangled from its cord, an obscene object in Salizar's vision. He took the phone, cursing the uncontrollable shaking of his hand. This wasn't happening, he told himself. He hadn't signed on for this.

"Tell Pinchinko his guests at the hotel aren't welcome in Manila. Anyone involved with them will be given permanent deportation. I'll know whether you relayed the message. Repeat that."

"I...who...I...don't know...."

"Repeat the message, deliver it to your master, or the next bullet has your name on it."

Salizar found his voice. He repeated the strange message, but the graveyard voice wasn't finished.

"When you contact Pinchinko, also tell him crime doesn't pay. Repeat that."

The young executive did, felt the bile squirming up into his throat. He was about to protest that he didn't know what in the hell the stranger was talking about, that he couldn't possibly insult the number-one man in NorAmAsian in that manner, when he heard the dial tone buzzing like some angry insect in his ear.

Alone, Salizar looked past his chair, through the opening in the front of the desk, stared at the partially decapitated Russian and vomited.

PUNCTUALITY and predictability. In short their greed killed them.

Eighty yards, give or take. Shooting down, with the wind at his back, two stationary targets in full view of the crosshairs of the Starlite scope, the Executioner had scored a double bull's-eye.

The sinister and secret world of NorAmAsian had just been dealt its third crushing blow, and the night was still young. But as far as Mack Bolan was concerned, it was only the beginning of ripping the legitimate face off a megacorporation that moved narcotics, pornography and human flesh in order to further its agenda of building a legitimate international monopoly, which ranged in everything from banking to computers to building aircraft to marketing the latest in computer software and video games.

The intel from Stony Man Farm that had put the Manila shopping list in Bolan's hand once again panned out. Yuri Voslov and Vladimir Dischinka lay dead in spreading pools of blood near the rising star of NorAmAsian.

The identities of the dead Russians in Salizar's office had already been confirmed—via faxed intel from Stony Man Farm, complete with photos—to be ex-KGB agents who were now envoys for the Russian Mafia in the Philippines. Somehow they were connected, did business with Kuschka—Bolan was sure of it. Too many coincidences were popping up in Manila. The players of NorAmAsian in Manila were clearly in collusion with Hydra, who, if nothing else, had given Bolan's enemies safe haven.

The Executioner removed the customized sound suppressor from the Remington 700 sniper rifle. The large briefcase that had carried the pieces of the rifle to the top of the hotel lay at Bolan's feet. He would go back the way he had come—down the service stairs, having already blown the lock off the door that led to the roof with a silenced 9 mm round from his Beretta, stroll out the lobby, bustling with all manner of international businessmen. No one would be the wiser that death had moved through their ranks.

Feeling the hot breeze on his face, the soldier checked out his latest work. Below and directly across from his rooftop vantage there was still no sign that Salizar was about to come out from behind his desk. It didn't matter. Salizar would be the third messenger boy for the two Stony Man warriors. The face of Manila crime and corruption was about to change forever. If nothing else, NorAmAsian would be exposed as a front for a major international criminal conspiracy, its founding fathers either dead or aiding Bolan in his hunt for the primary targets.

Bolan began to feel his CIA contacts in Manila were on the level. It was the CIA who knew about the Russian Mafia presence in Manila, knew all the

details about the biweekly pickup of cash from
NorAmAsian in the junior VP's office suite.

The soldier patched through to Grimaldi on his
handheld radio. He simply told his friend and ally,
"Their wings have been clipped. I'm coming down."

The Executioner got busy disassembling the sniper
rifle.

One more stop on the hit parade, and Bolan knew
the rats would be ready to come scurrying out of their
hole, to run straight into the Executioner's gun sights.

7

Something was more terribly wrong than ever. William McBain could smell it in the air, feel it in his belly, sense it in everything that had previously gone to hell, all the way from Manhattan to the south of France.

It was something palpably ominous, threatening in the utter silence of the shadows.

A little more than one hour after being dismissed, William McBain found himself once again front and center before the shadows. There was another shadow now present, tall and unmoving behind the blue light, at the far end of the table.

The talking shadow was again on the phone, only this time he was carrying on the conversation in English. McBain listened, felt the fear gnawing at his belly, squeezing acid slime up his chest.

"Yes... Yes. I understand. This is most disturbing news. No. I assure you we did not bring this trouble to your country. No. I have no idea why that is happening to you, only that it now threatens all of us. That much is clear to me."

Whatever was going on, McBain knew it wasn't good. Things were heating up past the boiling point; he could feel murder in the air.

"The general, as we all are, need I remind you, is

an honored guest in your hotel. I understand your concern. You have been paid handsomely, and the proper authorities are under your control and influence. What was that?''

McBain's gut rumbled, more acid churning. "Honored guest." The shadow was talking to Bernaldi Pinchinko, president of NorAmAsian. More problems. McBain knew his history with Pinchinko was just as sordid, muddied by intrigue and selfish motivations as his dealings with the Russians. But they were all tied in to the Coalition. In fact there was no escaping the Coalition. It was everywhere, it seemed.

Pinchinko's company, McBain knew, was founded by a group of Filipino and American businessmen, many of whom McBain had past dealings with, in both business and the pursuit of pleasure. NorAmAsian practically owned Manila, at least behind the scenes, namely running the entire heroin and sex trade, both nationally and internationally, with an iron hand and billion-dollar accounts, most of it in the World Bank Center. McBain was a major shareholder in the corporation, having been talked into investing in NorAmAsian in its beginnings by a former Army buddy—who was now in prison serving ten life sentences thanks to the late senator from New York—and by Calhoun.

NorAmAsian had been created, from the sidelines and the shadows, essentially by dirty money from rogue CIA agents, ex-KGB thugs who were in collusion with the Russian Mafia and assorted investors, like himself, who wanted to hide excess cash. Not to mention a long list of assorted international criminals, deposed dictators, bank presidents who had bilked investors, all wanting to stash their ill-gotten gains in NorAmAsian.

Given recent events, everything was on the verge of crumbling, legal or otherwise or in between. NorAmAsian fell into the in-between category. If NorAmAsian's operations in the States fell apart under the legal microscope of the Justice Department, heads would roll clear around the globe. Hell, whole companies and corporations that had seen leverage buyouts by NorAmAsian would be lining up before an outraged public, and a firing squad would be preferable to twenty life terms for the countless investors and shareholders in the corporation.

"Kindly do not panic.... What is that? Two men, you say?... Americans? Yes, I heard you. You have descriptions of these men?... They told you what?"

McBain stifled the oath, but couldn't keep the bile from squirting up his throat. Their nameless, relentless hunters had landed in Manila. The recurring nightmare was about to become reality. Again.

A little more conciliatory understanding from the shadow, then McBain heard the man put an edge to his voice. "You are to stay put. I will send six men.... No, you will do this my way. Have you forgotten who put your corporation on the international map?... I heard you. You have dead business associates and flunkies strewed all over the city, you have lost millions of dollars of merchandise, but listen to me. You must distance yourself at this time from those men who have been attacked, the ones who are relaying the messages of your attackers.... Yes, I understand you have suffered serious financial loss. You must put that behind you... They burned down a whorehouse? Forget him! I know of the man! He is just a pimp.

You will relieve yourself and myself of his existence immediately, and if you cannot do it, I will see to it personally.''

McBain couldn't believe what he was hearing. Much less that the shadow was having this give-and-take with Pinchinko about drugs, whores and assassination on a cellular telephone. Forget the scrambler, the least-sophisticated state-of-the-art eavesdropping devices could monitor the entire conversation.

Suddenly, as if taking some silent cue from the talker, McBain saw the tall shadow step from behind the table.

Petre Kuschka rolled out of the blue light.

"Comrade General." A cold smile. "You do not look so pleased to see me again."

McBain swallowed hard, saw something more menacing than ever in the ex-KGB assassin's black eyes. "Calhoun? Did he make it?"

"Comrade Major and what is left of his men are safe and close. Soon we will all be reunited, do not worry. I must inform you, however, we have suffered grave setbacks and the loss of many good soldiers, contacts and merchandise that was bought and paid for. You might say that at this time there is enough blame to go around for all of us."

Before McBain could pursue a line of questioning, the shadow barked one final order at Pinchinko. The man was to stay put. Assistance was on the way. He would have a chopper en route for Pinchinko's estate.

"Gentlemen," the shadow said, "it would appear the trouble you have had has found us in Manila. Perhaps you have already gathered, but that was Pinchinko, our main moneyman here in the Philippines. A lackey for the Coalition, nonetheless, but a man in our pocket who will ensure us one of our goals—if we get that far. Let me get you both up to speed. Two Americans have attacked his varied business interests in the past hour. A warehouse, burned to the ground, his hired gunmen killed. A warehouse that was moving large amounts of heroin, a good portion of which was destined for our comrades in Moscow. Further, a whorehouse was attacked and burned, again more merchandise that we have invested in. And now it would seem a sniper picked off two of our friends from Moscow and right in an upper-floor office of NorAmAsian. Two men. Hunting and killing the Coalition's frontline troops, dismantling our money sources, severing our crucial contacts and connections at will. Incredible as it sounds. Two men."

"They are here."

"But of course!" the shadow roared at Kuschka. "Gentlemen, whatever has gone before, whatever trouble you have had and why it has followed us to Manila must be dealt with right away. I know for a fact the CIA has this hotel under surveillance, but I do not believe these men are merely CIA black operatives."

"So why not just pack up and move on?" McBain asked.

"Are you insane, or just disloyal or a plain despicable coward?" the shadow bellowed. "Run and hide. We will not. These two men who have hunted and attacked you around the world are hunting us, Comrade General, and I cannot allow the trail of bodies to continue to follow us, leaving behind wounded prisoners for their interrogation as we move blithely onto our next objective. They know something, I am sure, of our plans if, as Comrade Kuschka has informed me, they have taken prisoners along the way. I am at this time delivering a message from my own superiors. We are to stand our ground here and confront these nameless adversaries, CIA or whatever they are. Or we are not to return home. And home, Comrade General, is deep inside Russia. I hope, if we survive an attack by this unknown opposition, and an attack is certain to come, that you have no qualms about spending the rest of your days in Mother Russia.''

They might as well have shot him on the spot. The idea he would spend the remainder of his life in Russia sent a wave of angry resentment through McBain. That wasn't part of the original bargain. No, he was promised an island paradise. Now he was going to hell on earth. But to protest, he knew, meant certain death. He lied. ''No. Either way, it would seem I have no choice,'' he said.

''That is the first honest, sensible thing I have heard come out of your mouth since laying eyes on you.''

Honesty, McBain bitterly thought, like hope, was in the heart of the beholder. Right then he knew it was all over but the crying—only someone else would be shedding the tears. The hunters would come, all right, and they would bring some new surprise that would again drop their world on them. When it hit the fan, McBain determined he would find a way to be free of the Russians. And, of course, get his hands on his stash, run like hell while they were all dying around him and not look back. No way would he ever spend his golden years, after all the suffering, setbacks, backstabbing he'd endured, in a cold, gray, grim, lifeless, joyless, pleasureless foreign land not of his choosing.

"All right, then," McBain asked the shadow, "just what is it you want us to do?"

The shadow took his time answering. "We wait right here for the enemy to come to us. We will hold our ground, go down to the last man, if necessary. I do not care if this entire hotel goes down in flames. If we fail, our lives are not worth shit anyway."

McBain silently cursed the day he'd ever been caught on tape with a swallow. He could almost see his life flash before his eyes.

BOLAN WALKED up the steps and settled onto a narrow landing that would lead to the office in the back of the nightclub. On the move, passing the little stages where nearly naked Filipinas shook and gyrated to American rock and roll, the Executioner scanned the club. Just inside a narrow archway he found Nor-AmAsian's youngest and finest executives, gathered in a booth, a few Filipinas lap-dancing or table-topping. The four suits were next on Bolan's agenda.

Below him, the soldier saw that the patrons of the Doll Cage Filipina were having a grand old time. The place was all glass, floor to ceiling, or teakwood and palm trees, with long bars on each side of the room. Even at that hour both the first and second floors were packed with the howling wolves and the eager dancers snatching up easy money. The more privileged were led upstairs to a series of rooms where even bigger and easier money changed hands. The grim-faced suits, however, at least six at first count, obviously packing heat beneath their suit jackets, caught the longest scrutiny from the Executioner.

Bolan spotted his backup, now settling himself onto a stool at the bar. Like Grimaldi, the soldier was toting a mini-Uzi beneath a loose-fitting windbreaker. The Executioner had spare clips for the minisubgun, plus the silenced Beretta and the Desert Eagle. He also carried two incendiary grenades, ready to burn down another house that NorAmAsian had built. According to intel from both Stony Man Farm and the CIA, Pinchinko had a chain of Doll Cage nightclubs, which NorAmAsian money had built. There was the Doll Cage Singapore, Doll Cage Taiwan, Doll Cage Tokyo. One in Honolulu, Los Angeles, New York, Miami. Of course, they were built to cater to the platinum-credit-card crowd, giving the surface appearance of fun and games for stressed-out execs or those with plenty of money to burn. Behind the mask, though, the clubs were moving and shaking NorAmAsian's other interests in drugs, prostitution, white slavery, money laundering. Of course, Bolan had neither the time nor the interest to hit every strip joint owned by Pinchinko. One would suffice.

In the interests of furthering his own campaign, Bolan had brought an empty briefcase with him for his unannounced meet with Ramos Echua, boss of Pinchinko's upper-crust Manila skin dive. He suspected the owner kept a serious stockpile of cash on hand. If that was true, then Bolan was going for a war chest, in case something came up at a later date and funds could be used to enlist services or weapons. The way the campaign was shaping up, Bolan suspected one or several more countries were set for an Executioner visit.

Time was running out either way in Manila, and Bolan knew he had to pick up the pace.

He saw two lean, long-haired Filipino hardmen in thousand-dollar suits, clearly packing large handguns beneath jackets step up from the shadow to greet him, all scowls and menacing eyes.

Maybe they sensed some clear and present threat in Bolan. Maybe every unannounced arrival coming for the office was greeted by blatant hostility and a show of force. Maybe bad news just simply traveled at the speed of light in this town.

Whatever, they were digging for hardware when the Executioner beat them to it. He let their .357 Magnum pistols clear their jackets, then shot them both with a silenced 9 mm round right between the eyes.

For the Doll Cage Filipina, the party was over.

8

Beretta leading the way, Bolan hit the open door to the office at the end of the hall. He spotted the security camera on the ceiling, then heard the soft beep of someone punching a cellular phone just inside the doorway. The jig was up. Crouched, the soldier went in low and hard, took in the large, posh office in an eye blink, Beretta poised for any and all comers.

No sign of gun-toting thugs.

Bolan focused on the desperate face of Ramos Echua with the phone just about to reach his ear. The soldier blasted the phone out of Echua's hand and took off a thumb in the process. The Executioner didn't give Echua time for the horror and pain to sink in as blood and plastic shrapnel hit the club owner in the face. Two long strides and Bolan stood over the club boss.

A quick search of the office showed Bolan a bank of security cameras mounted to the ceiling. He didn't see any of the goon squad move from their various positions around the first or second floors. It also looked as if they were alone in the office. Even still, Bolan wasn't about to trust anything to first appearances. Soon enough all hell was going to break loose. The easy part was getting in.

"I'll get right to the point," the soldier growled,

grabbing Echua's ponytail and yanking his head back, pressing the silenced snout of the Beretta under his chin. "I need money. Play ball, you'll live through the night. You don't, you'll lose a lot more than just a thumb. Nod if you intend to cooperate."

Bolan believed he reached the man as Echua nodded. The soldier kept the guy's hair locked in a fist while Echua indicated where the safe was.

"Use your good hand. I don't need you bleeding all over my money," Bolan said, then let the man bend to pull back a piece of carpet under the desk, then dial open the floor safe. The soldier glanced at the door, the cameras, ready to pump one in the back of Echua's head if he pulled something other than money out of the hole.

It was a sizable donation. Bolan released Echua, opened the briefcase, then ordered the man to fill it. When his war chest was stuffed with stacks of hundred-dollar bills, Bolan snatched the man from under the desk, jacked him toward the doorway.

Now the toughest part.

"You're going to have a fire," Bolan told Echua. "You will quickly clear everyone out of the building. You will run around and scream 'fire.' Once I leave, you will call Pinchinko. Tell him a close friend of General McBain ripped him off."

"You're a dead man, whoever you are."

"I've been hearing that all night. So far I'm still breathing."

He peered into the hall, saw it was clear and shoved Echua forward. Once the crowd was clearing the club, Bolan would unleash an incendiary bomb back down the hall. The human stampede would provide the escape route for the Stony Man duo. Easier said than done. It was dicey all around. The hired thugs could spot Bolan with the gun and start blasting away, indifferent to innocent bystanders. But the soldier had already laid out the plan to Grimaldi. The security men were to be taken out before they could make their play.

They reached the doorway, and Bolan told Echua, "Do it. Make it believable. If you don't, I have no problem putting one in your back."

Echua complied.

Then the unexpected happened. Echua was screaming "Fire! Fire! Everyone clear the building," when Bolan sensed movement from behind.

The sound of a subgun cutting loose flayed the air behind Bolan, but the Executioner was already through the doorway. So a goon had been lying in wait, somewhere in the office or the hallway.

Bolan saw the human stampede begin in earnest, heading for the far stairway. Echua was holding up his end of the charade when the second problem showed.

The goon at the far end of the second floor was barreling his way through the surging mob of suits and naked skin, a large handgun coming up and tracking the big American when Bolan beat him to it. One 9 mm round chugged from the Beretta, coring through the goon's forehead, the impact spinning him where he did a nosedive over the rail.

The Executioner heard the distant chatter of the subgun, bullets raking the doorjamb. He judged the enemy was staying put, probably waiting for reinforcements.

With no better time to begin to burn down the Doll

Cage, Bolan primed the grenade, wheeled and pitched it down the hall.

THE TENSE WAITING came to the brutal and loud end Grimaldi was anticipating. At first the plan fell into place, with Echua hollering "Fire," then the inevitable human stampede.

Next came the sound of automatic weapons fire, the big guy ducking inside the doorway upstairs, before a goon was nailed by Bolan on the opposite end of the floor.

Now they were scurrying, hollering and cursing everywhere, and Grimaldi got to work selecting targets, grimly intent on wiping out the security force. The explosion upstairs told the ace pilot Bolan had blown a wave of white phosphorous through the hallway. The ensuing scream of a man being burned alive confirmed it.

From his position near the end of the bar, Grimaldi unleathered his own silenced Beretta 93-R. The bartender came up with a Heckler & Koch MP-5 subgun and was moving from behind the bar when Grimaldi nailed him one through the brain.

The Stony Man pilot searched out another goon, found one bursting up the steps in an attempt to come up on Bolan's rear. Grimaldi sighted down, caressed the trigger and fired a single 9 mm Parabellum round that drilled into the back of the goon's skull. The guy toppled back, rolling down the steps.

Grimaldi took in the pandemonium on the first floor. They were running, bowling one another over in a mad scramble for the front doors.

Figure six goons, according to intel, and Grimaldi knew that at least four were down for the count.

Unfortunately intel didn't pan out on the numbers.

They came charging out of the upstairs rooms, bounding down the steps, girls, johns and gunners. At least four more subgun-wielding hardmen made the scene than were expected.

Too bad for them.

As they raced across the first floor, wild eyes locked on the upstairs, Grimaldi sheathed the Beretta, drew the mini-Uzi. He would have less control with the compact subgun than the Beretta, but the moment called for multiple quick kills.

From the corner of his eye, Grimaldi caught the slick ball of fire licking out from the second-floor hall. The place was set to burn quick. White phosphorous clung like glue to anything it touched and showed no mercy.

Stepping away from the bar, Grimaldi waited until he got a momentary clear field of fire. Two of the four hardmen stood out between the surging throng long enough for the Stony Man pilot to cut loose with the mini-Uzi, hose them down with 9 mm death.

So far it looked as if innocent patrons were making the doors.

Grimaldi had other concerns as the surviving two gunners sought him out, spotted him and opened up. Glass shattered behind the ace pilot as their subguns tracked on. A man in a business suit cried out. The goons didn't care whom they nailed as long as they took care of the immediate threat to their club, their boss, their jobs. The two Stony Man warriors had hoped it wouldn't come to that. It only told Grimaldi these guys regarded noncombatants with utter callousness.

Unfortunately the enemy had gotten the bead on

Grimaldi. Bullets whizzed dangerously close over his head, and he was forced to dive for cover behind a table, overturning it and bringing it down as a shield to their autofire as bullets gouged the wood. The shrill screams went on, a deafening assault to Grimaldi's ears.

As he peered around the corner, taking his chances, both gunmen were sent tumbling back. Double sprays of blood jetted for a heartbeat from their shattered skulls.

Score two more for the home team.

Checking his rear, finding no new threat, Grimaldi headed for the doorway. He spotted Bolan descending the far steps. Time to bolt.

It was also time to ensure the club would burn completely. Grimaldi found the area behind him vacant of fleeing patrons. He armed an incendiary grenade and opted for the bar, looking to ignite alcohol, more insurance. He lobbed the steel egg, then met Bolan in the foyer.

The grenade blew another nail in the coffin of NorAmAsian.

But Grimaldi knew what lay ahead. So far the Manila blitz had gone off without a hitch.

The worst, he knew, was yet to come. He could feel the home stretch just around the next corner. And if things had been bloody, brutal and ugly up to now, they were about to exceed what had gone before tenfold. The enemy, after all, was still alive and kicking, even in its death throes.

Grimaldi swiftly moved alongside Bolan, melting into the rear of the mob and heading out into the night.

"I DON'T KNOW who you two are, what agency you work for, but you've just trampled all over a major Company operation. I've given you everything you've asked for, you move my people out of our own private airfield, I give you a Huey, intelligence out the wazoo and now you're running amok all over Luzon, kicking up more shit than this island has seen since World War II."

Bolan looked at the CIA agent. The tall, crew-cut operative named Culmore stood in the soft glow of the overhead light in the belly of the Huey. Bolan didn't have time to listen to the guy's squawking. Something didn't fit, he sensed, with the CIA in Manila. Stony Man Farm had its own elaborate and foolproof intelligence network, equal to or better than the CIA, DIA, maybe even the Pentagon. That the CIA was suddenly showing up wherever the two warriors went meant one of two things to Bolan. First CIA black-bag operation was buried so deep that all manner of illegalities and cutthroat activity was blessed by someone in charge who believed he was the only higher authority. The end result was that no one on either side knew who was who or what was what.

Second it was a renegade operation, and rogue agents were running about, maybe protecting the interests of Calhoun, McBain, Kuschka. If that was the case, then Bolan intended to flush out any traitors he could find along the way. The latter was why he'd let Culmore tag along.

However it was sliced, Culmore and his stakeout team at the New Hotel Manila were new factors, brought in, given their orders via Brognola's CIA contacts. Theirs was not to question why.

Sitting on the bench, the roar of rotors filling the

tight silence, Bolan checked his weapons. Everything was loaded, ready to go: full clip in the M-16, M-203 grenade launcher loaded with a 40 mm grenade. He was outfitted in a combat blacksuit, harness, earpiece and throat mike, spare clips for the Beretta, .44 Magnum Desert Eagle, assault rifle grenades and other weapons of his trade. While the spook growled and glared, Bolan went to work with black war paint, covering every exposed part, face, neck, hands.

The intel on numbers and security of Pinchinko's estate was already laid out by his CIA contact. The president of NorAmAsian had a beach villa on the China Sea, an isolated compound, about eleven miles north of Subic Bay. Shortly that estate would change forever. In fact its owner would be lucky if even one wall was left standing when the next phase had been completed.

"Let's get something straight, Culmore. You insisted on coming along," Bolan said. "I relented because I still need some intelligence on the hotel, since you people have been inside, watching my targets for I don't know how long. If you have questions about us, it doesn't matter. What I've seen is the CIA cropping up wherever I go. They've known about Calhoun, McBain, the whole KGB–Russian Mafia connection for some time. Only now somebody's doing something about it."

"By killing them at will? Unraveling two years of intelligence work and just when we're about to drop the net over these guys?"

More pieces of the puzzle didn't fit to Bolan. The soldier was sure the agent was blowing smoke. If they were that close, had known all along about the WBC, NorAmAsian, McBain, the others, they would have dropped the net by now. He recalled the black-operations teams that had shown up, without warning, in Lebanon and Pakistan. Thanks to Brognola's clout, Bolan and Grimaldi had gotten on board just before it was set to hit the fan. Perhaps those black-ops teams had been acting on their own, grabbing up the money and the goods for themselves—only the U.S. military had taken down the Pakistani ship with its nuclear cargo. In the shadow world the CIA lived in, Bolan knew better than to trust anything at face value.

Whatever had gone before was done. Focus on the moment. The scam artists, the cutthroats, the renegades would be found out and stamped out soon enough. Whether it was done Bolan's way or by legal means, sooner or later the whole conspiracy was going to come to a grinding end, with guys thrashing and squealing on one another, or the enemy at one another's throats.

Bolan glanced at the 9 mm Glock pistol in Culmore's shoulder holster, the Uzi subgun slung across his shoulder. If the guy wanted in, well, Bolan was going solo, with Grimaldi providing the air support. If the so-called operative was in some way part of the opposition, then no amount of hardware would save him.

Suddenly Grimaldi patched through on Bolan's handheld radio. "Yeah," the soldier answered.

"I can see the lights on the compound, eleven o'clock, about two miles and closing."

"You know what to do," Bolan stated.

"Roger, I'll let you know when I find a suitable drop site."

"You guys are crazy."

Bolan looked at his CIA contact. "Is that right?"

For a moment he wasn't sure what he saw in the man's eyes. But the gaze narrowed, and something flickered in the stare that Bolan couldn't quite read. The soldier let all of the questions he could have put to the operative ride. He had what he needed. For now, he knew the hotel's top floor was occupied by McBain and maybe twenty-five Russians. Whether they were ex-KGB, Russian Mafia, it didn't matter. They were next, and hopefully, last on Bolan's Manila hit parade.

What Bolan did know was the layout of the hotel, that two floors beneath the enemy's lair were vacant. He wasn't sure what that meant, only that McBain and his coconspirators had control of the hotel. Bolan had in mind what he hoped was the final blitzing surprise for the enemy.

"So, I just stay put in this chopper while you two raise hell?"

"If I need you, I'll call you," Bolan said.

"Indulge me one item."

"What?"

"I want Pinchinko alive. The guy has invaluable information about this Russian connection in the Philippines."

No doubt. Bolan wanted Pinchinko alive, too, but for other reasons. The man was going to be grilled for whatever he knew about McBain and the Russian connection, but he would also be Bolan's human shield, a ticket into the New Hotel Manila, all the way to the top floor. Never one to pull punches, this time out, Bolan would drive it, head-on, and all the way down the enemy's throat.

"That all depends," Bolan said, letting Culmore sweat it out.

"On what?"

"On Pinchinko."

Culmore grumbled an oath but didn't pursue it.

The gunship banked to starboard. Grimaldi patched through. It was just about time to take on NorAm-Asian's president.

Their Filipino connection was having obvious difficulty coping with the crisis. It was to be expected, Petre Kuschka thought, running a long finger over the scars on his face, inflicted by flying shrapnel from exploding mines and grenades from distant wars or small conflicts fought in what seemed a thousand lifetimes ago. The multibillionaire head of NorAmAsian might have believed himself in charge of something, but Kuschka knew the truth. Bernaldi Pinchinko was the Coalition's front moneyman in the Pacific Rim. His money had bought all the right contacts, scarfed up land from Luzon to Borneo, but his company was mostly built on ill-gotten gains from rogue intelligence players on both sides of the former iron curtain—not to mention major narcotics traffickers and other billionaire criminals who had dumped considerable fortunes into NorAmAsian. Not only did they thus hide their wealth, but they also at the same time accumulated interest through the World Bank Center, giving Kuschka and the Coalition a sizable piece of their deposits as contracted—along with a little stealing, by means of an electronic touch, here and there, from numbered bank accounts.

Their Filipino connection was having obvious difficulty coping with the crisis. It was to be expected, Petre Kuschka thought, running a long finger over the scars on his face, inflicted by flying shrapnel from exploding mines and grenades from distant wars or small conflicts fought in what seemed a thousand lifetimes ago. The multibillionaire head of NorAmAsian might have believed himself in charge of something, but Kuschka knew the truth. Bernaldi Pinchinko was the Coalition's front moneyman in the Pacific Rim. His money had bought all the right contacts, scarfed up land from Luzon to Borneo, but his company was mostly built on ill-gotten gains from rogue intelligence players on both sides of the former iron curtain—not to mention major narcotics traffickers and other billionaire criminals who had dumped considerable fortunes into NorAmAsian. Not only did they thus hide their wealth, but they also at the same time accumulated interest through the World Bank Center, giving Kuschka and the Coalition a sizable piece of their deposits as contracted—along with a little stealing, by means of an electronic touch, here and there, from numbered bank accounts.

So Pinchinko was merely a puppet on the string, clueless as to what was really soon to happen in the

Philippines. Pinchinko was grist for the Hydra mill, here today, gone tomorrow, concerned only about his wealth and pleasure. Soon the Philippines would become a major springboard from which the Coalition would launch its assault on the so-called free world. And what was stored in the jungles of Borneo—where Kuschka had also left Calhoun and the Americans some twelve hours ago before jetting on to a private airfield south of Manila—would provide the spearhead for a revolution of horror, chaos and total anarchy that would eventually leave the Coalition in supreme rule of the Philippines, threatening other Asian counties to the north with total annihilation.

But Pinchinko was only one reason why Kuschka was by the man's side, in the dead of night, with fifteen heavily armed former Spetsnaz troops. They were rounding up the man's guests—mostly women and playboys of the senior-executive circle privy to these pleasure bashes—herding them into one of the three executive choppers on the tarmac. No, the former KGB assassin was on the man's beachfront compound to confront and eliminate the two hunters who had landed in Manila. Once and for all, Kuschka would take out the two men who had attacked them repeatedly, wiped out arms and drug deals. Revenge was demanded. If they came in attack aircraft again, well, that was what the RPG-7 rocket launchers were for.

"What is the meaning of these attacks? Who are these men? Two men, just 'two' men who are destroying my businesses around me, killing my people at will, even sniping off your own people and in my own office building in Manila, burning down my warehouses and stockpiles of merchandise I cannot so easily replace! I just received a call that my nightclub was attacked and burned to the ground. I have lost millions this night. This is an outrage! The police, and I don't care how many I own in my pocket, will come to me with many questions I cannot answer. Well? Don't stand there like a piece of stone. I want answers.''

Kuschka didn't flinch in the face of Bernaldi Pinchinko's outrage. Instead, he stood like stone, inspecting the sprawling grounds of the villa. And listening to the night. There. Somewhere from the south, then fading to the east, a faint whapping bleat. What was that? A chopper?

The Russian tensed, ignoring Pinchinko's blathering. They were grouped on the southwest lawn, near the motor pool, just beyond the helipad. Most of the man's security—motion sensors, cameras, watchdogs and sentries—was limited to the immediate area around or inside the villa proper. All around the villa, beyond the pool, gazebo, tennis courts, the driveway was open ground, giving way to the sandy beach and the China Sea beyond to the west, then lush tropical vegetation north, east and south. The floodlights were barely strong enough to throw more than shadows on the wall of trees and shrubbery that nearly completely ringed the perimeter. And with the beach nearly tucked up against the villa, anyone could come up on the compound after hitting the shore in a motorboat. The man had no common sense when it came to protecting himself, much less the Coalition's agenda. Pinchinko obviously figured a few thugs with guns could protect his life.

Well, Kuschka was there to save the night, the Coalition and his own future. He knew it was coming down to another brutal engagement very soon, right there on Pinchinko's compound; he could feel it in his bones. This time he was ready, and his orders were explicit. It didn't trouble him that the Coalition had sent Major General Levi Turbov, formerly of the VGK, the Soviet Supreme High Command, to Manila. Kuschka had known all along that he would have had to contact his superiors and inform them of the setbacks, crises and fiascos they had suffered. Well, the major general was safe for the moment behind his blue light in McBain's hotel suite, giving out orders, making McBain sweat through the night, wondering if he would see another sunrise. But if Kuschka failed to crush the two Americans away from the hotel he knew that blue light would soon be awash in the blood from a few of his superiors on the board of directors. Already the plan was to move on to Borneo and begin to ship out the hot agents, which was another reason why the Coalition had sent out the generals. That couldn't possibly happen, though, if the trouble that had haunted him since Colombia was not permanently laid to rest in Manila.

And CIA surveillance of the hotel? So the major general was concerned about the CIA crawling all over Manila, staking out the hotel, monitoring their moves. The major general didn't know that Kuschka already had his own CIA contact, covering their moves, updating them on the sly. And Kuschka knew exactly who was kicking Pinchinko's behind all over Manila.

The Russian snugged the AK-47 higher up on his shoulder. He was sweating in his black turtleneck. Part of his burden was voluntary and certainly necessary. The hunters he was sure would come for Pinchinko were professional killers; their bullets so far had flown straight and true. Kuschka wasn't taking any chances.

Behind him the chopper with its noncombatants lifted off, leaving the two executive choppers that ferried in Kuschka and his troops on the tarmac. The night was warm, the air tinged with salt that was carried on a soft wind from the beach. Soon he wanted only to smell the blood of his enemies in the air.

Finally Kuschka addressed the short, mustachioed Pinchinko. "I suggest you stand by my side at all times."

"What are we waiting for? These two men who are seeking to ruin me?"

"I would be more concerned about my ruin, Comrade Pinchinko. What is bad for me will be equally bad for you."

"Take your threats and shove them up your ass. Are you forgetting you've been using my planes, my airfield in Borneo, my hotel, my contacts, my protection?"

"Your cooperation will not go unrewarded."

There. Kuschka heard it, made out the sound of a chopper, flying east, but now coming back from the north. He smiled, felt his blood race, his temples throb.

The hunters had arrived.

Kuschka ignored Pinchinko's insistent questions, crushed the urge to slap the Filipino to the ground and began to bark out the orders.

This time Kuschka was ready to finally see his enemies dead at his feet.

IT WAS A SCARRED DEMON'S face that Mack Bolan had mentally filed away and, more importantly, wanted to blow away since first seeing it in Colombia.

From his position north of the compound, near the edge of the treeline, Bolan observed the scar-faced assassin's lips move in the tunneled vision of his infrared, high-powered binoculars. The ex-KGB assassin was barking orders, and Bolan saw three armed shadows fall out in a skirmish line, headed his way.

The Executioner had waited long enough anyway. Ten minutes earlier, Grimaldi had dropped off the soldier in a clearing, two hundred yards to the rear. The ace pilot was now flying south, ready for Bolan to patch through and give the order to come in, low and hard, blasting anything that moved with a weapon.

Only this time around Bolan saw his CIA contact had neglected to mention one critical item. The enemy had choppers grounded on the tarmac on the southwest part of the compound. One of those choppers was already flying south, in the direction of Manila. Through his field glasses, the soldier had already glimpsed the frightened faces of women, guys in suits or various states of undress, maybe others who were hired help. Pinchinko, whom Bolan had spotted standing beside Kuschka and engaging the Russian killer in a one-way argument, was a young bachelor with no children. If nothing else, the premises had been cleared of noncombatants.

Still, Culmore would know that Grimaldi would take out first and foremost anything the enemy might attempt an escape in, car or chopper. An oversight? So far, Culmore had filled Bolan and Grimaldi in on every detail of every hit. Almost too good, in some ways, as if the guy had been on the inside the whole time, holding hands with the enemy. Suddenly the pieces were fitting together in Bolan's mind where Culmore was concerned.

The soldier concentrated on the three hunters coming for him. Someone had obviously heard or spotted the chopper. So be it. Bolan knew that taking the enemy by complete surprise this time was out of the question.

Thus the Huey with its XM-21 weapons system. It was an old gunship, but the Huey was still a favorite all over the world to ferry the CIA. Earlier, with a little help from the blacksuits flown in from the Farm, Grimaldi had given the gunship a thorough preflight check. It would do.

Bolan swiftly and silently moved deeper into the forest, his gaze locked on the middle hunter moving directly toward him. A silent, invisible shadow, Bolan crouched in the brush, waiting for them to come to him.

They did. The Executioner slid the Ka-bar fighting knife free from its sheath. He could have opted for the silenced Beretta, but he wanted the first one as up close and personal as possible, shave the odds before going to work with the Beretta. The middle shadow, unwittingly on a collision course with death, walked right past Bolan's hiding place in the brush. Out of the corner of his eye, Bolan saw the flanking shadows vanish from their comrade's sight behind a wall of trees. There would never be a more perfect opportunity.

The Executioner sprang on the shadow from behind. It was over in less than two seconds. One hand wrapped around his victim's mouth, Bolan drove the blade deep and hard across the throat, severing jugular, windpipe, the works. The Russian released his

AK-47, tried to claw for Bolan's face for a brief moment, then went limp in the soldier's grasp. Bolan quietly laid his victim in the brush, wiped the knife off on the dead Russian's pantleg.

"Dryvich?"

Dropping on his haunches, Bolan sheathed the blade, drew the Beretta. Rustling sounded on his flanks. The two stalkers were close, moving parallel to each other, calling out for their dead comrade. There was just enough light hitting the forest edge from the compound to let Bolan adjust to their figures without aid of NVD goggles. Two shadows, fifteen yards to either side, broke from the wall of vegetation. They knew something was wrong.

One chance was all Bolan would get. Either way, when they didn't report back to Kuschka, the alarms would still be sounded.

From his crouch the Executioner sighted on the shadow to his left, caressed the trigger. The chugging retort alerted the last shadow, but by then it was too late. Bolan scored a head shot, then wheeled and gave the Beretta a double tap. He nailed the shadow in the chest, flinging him back into the brush.

Unfortunately the shadow's AK-47 stammered out a burst before he crumpled to the ground.

Bolan got on his handheld radio. "Striker to Skywatcher, come in."

When the earpiece crackled with Grimaldi's voice, Bolan said, "I've been blown—fly in and let it rip."

"Affirm—"

Bolan heard sudden silence on the other end except for the faint sound of rotors coming over his transmission—and the clear sound of the bolt on a submachine gun being cocked.

Then the soldier heard his worst suspicions about Culmore become reality as Grimaldi said, "Culmore, you want to tell me why you have your Uzi pointed at me?"

The transmission abruptly ended. Bolan gritted his teeth, felt his blood run hot with anger. Dammit! The snakes had shown their fangs.

Bolan knew he was powerless to help his friend. They were both on their own.

The Executioner moved ahead, hoping for the best for Grimaldi, but fearing the worst. Either way, he would see the treacherous CIA agent pay up.

Right then, Bolan had a full plate from which to feast. Four armed shadows were already racing away from the compound.

He moved to the edge of the tree line, hunkered down and pulled the M-16 off his shoulder.

"FACE FRONT and set this bird down, asshole!"

Grimaldi kept staring over his shoulder at Culmore. For some reason, given all the treachery and backstabbing they had seen so far, all the riddles inside riddles, Grimaldi wasn't surprised he was facing a CIA traitor, staring into the muzzle of the man's Uzi.

Calm, searching his mind for some way out and coming up with a plan as risky as hell, the pilot said, "We're flying at two hundred feet, at almost two hundred miles per hour. You shoot me, we could go down in a hell of a hurry. Can you fly?"

"I'll do what I have to do."

Grimaldi had straightened out the course, was now flying back for the compound, which he figured was less than two minutes and closing. From the sound of it, Bolan was already engaged with the enemy.

"I overheard some of your conversation earlier. Is this what you meant by the two of us trampling all over a major CIA operation?"

Culmore bared his teeth. All right, Grimaldi thought, hand tightening on the cyclic stick, the rotor wash pounding through the open fuselage doorway slashing his face, the bastard was just to the right.

"A rogue operation, flyboy. I've got my own people inside what you think are the good guys. I was already briefed on the storm coming east—that's you two. I fed you two all the right intel, hoping I would lead you right into the guns. You're either good or you're lucky. I didn't expect you two to get this far."

"So you're part of McBain's team."

"Fuck McBain. We've known about McBain for years. What a few of us want is a little piece of what's left of an ever shrinking pie."

"And the Russians are going to give that to you?"

"Set it down! Now!"

Grimaldi nodded, braced himself and rolled the dice. In a smooth, rapid movement he pulled back on the cyclic stick. He glimpsed the anger and surprise hardening Culmore's expression as the nose went up and sent the rogue agent tumbling out of the cockpit. Even as the Uzi flamed and stuttered, 9 mm Parabellum rounds drilling spiderweb cracks in the Plexiglas windshield, Grimaldi stepped on the right rudder. Behind, riding the dip, he found the guy was rolling, screaming, firing at the ceiling from the fuselage, all arms and legs and vented mouth and bulging eyes. Bullets whined off the hull around Grimaldi as he rolled the bird still more to the starboard side and sent Culmore flailing and shrieking out into the night.

Quickly Grimaldi checked the instrument panel. He

blessed the fickle gods of fate, finding everything was undamaged.

Dead ahead, he saw the Pinchinko compound loom into view.

Once again it was show time. The Stony Man pilot manned the gun stick to the mounted 7.62 mm minigun and dipped the gunship down for a long, low strafing run.

10

If they were night-vision-detection ready, Bolan knew he could be tagged before he got out of the starting gate.

They weren't.

The Executioner was sliding through the forest, catching breaks in the brush where he could, silently angling up on the edge of the tree line when the four-some cut loose with AK-47 autofire. They swept the tree line where the brief stutter of their dead com-rade's weapon had alerted them. It proved a fatal guess for the Russians.

Bolan rolled up their flank, holding back on the trigger of the M-16, hosing them down with 5.56 mm lead tumblers, cutting a deadly figure eight from left to right, tearing into them until the clip was expended. No sooner were they pitching to the soft earth than Bolan geared up for the hard charge across a fifty-yard stretch of no-man's-land, when the familiar sound of rotors parted the night.

Air-fire support. Reprieve. And his friend had come out the other side of whatever had gone down with Culmore.

Swooping on the compound from the south, Bolan saw Grimaldi give the ground forces a lightning taste of death from the night sky. Rocket pods flamed and the minigun ripped free, electrically controlled, sizzling lines of 7.62 mm slugs chewing through the shadows scurrying around the motor pool and the helicopters. The sounds of glass shattering, explosions rocking the night, men screaming and igniting gas tanks created total hell on earth.

No one was leaving. Death ruled the night.

M-16 poised, and with a fresh 30-round magazine rammed home, Bolan broke cover. He charged from the tree line, angling for the pool, which was seeing a sudden rain of debris.

Without warning, the choppers erupted in blinding fireballs as Grimaldi scored big. Another line of sizzling rockets crushed at least half of the motor pool, sending metal and flesh in all directions.

Bolan spotted a problem, and not a second too soon.

A two-man RPG-7 rocket team was crouched by the pool, twin shadows by a palm tree, outlined in the Executioner's gun sights by the wavering umbrella of firelight from the motor pool. M-16 stammering, Bolan hit them from behind just as they were drawing a bead on the black shape of the Huey. The gunship soared past the back end of the villa, streaking out over open terrain. With Bolan's autofire kicking the rocket team poolside, their rockets chugged, flew wide. From somewhere at roughly eleven o'clock, another shadow ripped free with an AK-47, a line of slugs kicking up divots of soft earth on Bolan's heels. As fate had it, a piece of wreckage dropped from the sky and bowled the hardman down. As he made a shaky attempt to climb to his feet, Bolan poured it on the gunman, flung him back with a 3-round burst to the chest.

Intense firelight revealed more armed shadows, fleeing for their lives, as wreckage from the sky hammered the compound grounds.

Bolan wanted to bag Pinchinko, but if the NorAmAsian president bit the dust, it would simply open a void that the soldier would fill in some other way.

The New Hotel Manila was next, no matter what, and Bolan would hit the top floor, guns blazing, with or without the help of Pinchinko.

Combat senses on full alert, the Executioner glimpsed the Huey as it went into a hairpin turn near the tree line. He gave silent thanks that Grimaldi was still in the fray.

Either way, Bolan was going in hard.

First surveillance had showed Bolan there were fifteen to twenty gunmen, give or take. Now he figured the enemy force was depleted to at least half that number, maybe a few wounded stragglers.

Bolan saw figures scrambling for what was left of the motor pool. Somebody was looking to get out of there.

No such luck. Time to crank up the heat even more.

The Executioner took out two hardmen with a quick burst of 5.56 mm lead, stitching them up the spine, then went to work with the M-203. As the wreckage from the initial explosions started to settle, Bolan hit a crouch beside the ivy-trellised gazebo. He triggered the M-203, watched it sail on a true line, impact dead center into a limousine the size of a small boat. The explosion rocked the air, hurling metal and a human corpse into the side of the villa, punching out a gaping hole in the wall.

Bolan surged ahead. A familiar scarred face broke

into sight through the firewall. Kuschka was clutching Pinchinko by the shoulder.

There was a strange moment when Bolan met Kuschka's dark stare. The Russian assassin appeared to grin, fire nearly kissing his scarred visage. As if Pinchinko were nothing more than a sack of garbage, Kuschka flung him away and brought his AK-47 up and tracking.

Bolan held back on the M-16's trigger, then realized something was wrong from behind and cut his fire short. Grimaldi had spotted something to Bolan's flank, and the soldier heard the minigun stammering from behind and above. Bullets snapped around the Executioner, but the soldier was already moving to one side, diving for cover behind the jagged teeth of a smoking piece of debris.

Kuschka's line of fire ripped up the earth by Bolan, who came out of his roll. Confident Grimaldi had wiped out any threat behind him, the soldier searched out the tall shape of Kuschka. The Russian had darted behind a wall of fire, his AK-47 blazing, bullets punching holes in the sheet of flames. Bolan cut loose with his M-16, going for a chest shot. He was rewarded a heartbeat later by Kuschka's sharp cry of pain, the Russian's AK-47 chattering skyward.

Bolan nailed the ex-KGB assassin in the chest with another 3-round burst, and Kuschka pitched out of sight behind the firewall.

The Huey blew over Bolan. The gunship hovered over the lake of fire that consumed the motor pool and choppers. A quick scan of the hellgrounds, the windows of the villa and Bolan found nothing moving.

Except the president of NorAmAsian.

Bolan sprinted up to Pinchinko, who was a quivering mass of fear. After a glance at Kuschka's unmoving form, the soldier hauled Pinchinko up and jacked him toward the Huey as Grimaldi set the gunship down.

When he boarded the helicopter with his prisoner, Bolan looked at the grim set to Grimaldi's features. There was no sign of Culmore.

"What happened to Culmore?" Bolan asked his friend.

"He couldn't fly."

"You're going to have to cut Pinchinko loose eventually, but I think you already know that, Striker. Security reasons, that is."

They were flying at roughly five hundred feet, streaking over the dark, forested hill country, a dark plug of a volcano passing beneath the gunship as Grimaldi headed them inland.

Bolan looked out the open fuselage doorway as he spoke on the radio with Brognola. He had raised the big Fed on their agreed-upon, secured international frequency as soon as they had lifted off from the killzone of the Pinchinko compound. Grimaldi was en route for the CIA airfield now controlled by the Farm's blacksuits. Refuel, rearm, then it was on to the New Hotel Manila. Bolan would lay out the strike plan to Grimaldi when they were airborne again. It would be simple, and ugly. The Executioner intended to blow the enemy right off the roof of the hotel.

Right now Bolan was looking to get Brognola up to speed, and did it as quickly and accurately as possible. When the Justice man heard about the havoc they had wreaked, that their CIA contact turned out to be working for the opposition, he heaved a deep breath, then whistled. At that point, though, there wasn't much to be said, or done, except to keep on with the fight. They were on the threshold of wiping out the enemy.

Even still the night weighed on Bolan, the fatigue of combat, the globe-trotting hunt, rooting out and eliminating each and every new element in the conspiracy. And he could hear the worry and grim concern in Brognola's voice. The toughest part was yet to come, and both men knew it. At some point, Bolan believed it was going to end somewhere in Russia. Everything pointed toward the former Soviet Union, the KGB–Russian Mafia connection.

Over his headphones Bolan heard Brognola inform him that Stony Man Farm's satellite recon had pinpointed a remote airfield in the jungles of Borneo where air traffic had been monitored, coming in recently from a straight line from Pakistan. Kuschka's private jet, no doubt.

Bolan looked around. Rotor wash pounded through the belly of the gunship. Pinchinko was handcuffed and sat on the bench, his expression alternating between a scowl and a mask of terror. Bolan weighed Brognola's words, knew the big Fed was right about Pinchinko. The Justice Department would wait for another day when they could move on NorAmAsian and legally dismantle the corporation. If Pinchinko survived the night, then he would soon be faced with a list of criminal indictments that would bring his corporation crashing down. The list of employees that were either going to jail or finding themselves soon unemployed, reached across the Pacific, well into some of the bigger names of corporate America.

Briefly Bolan recalled what Grimaldi had told him about Culmore. It didn't surprise the Executioner that the CIA agent was on the opposing team. All it meant was that Bolan and Grimaldi were completely on their own the rest of the time in Manila. So be it. They had been on their own since the beginning of the campaign, more or less.

"Okay, so we've established the obvious, this connection between the Russian Mafia, former KGB agents, rogue elements of our own military and intelligence agencies." Brognola was thinking out loud, trying to make the pieces fit. "That this renegade operation has gone on for so long and is now coming full cycle, Striker, means that we've got people on our own side still crawling around and holding hands with the devil. How many Culmores are lurking around, I can't say.

"Item. As we speak, two of the former top brass the late senator put away are singing to the CIA, the NSA, DIA, you name it. The usual reduced sentences in accordance to what they know and who they can chop off at the knees. The songbirds also indicated that they helped arrange an extortion ring where nuclear physicists, scientists, and chem-war specialists from both here and in Russia either sold secrets or their services to this Hydra. A few of them are being put under the microscope now. Others have just vanished into thin air supposedly, according to the latest gathering of songbirds, disappeared into some remote secret installation in the Russian Far East. I'll get back to you on that when I learn more.

"As for your end, you've knocked out a lot of the opposition, and the wreckage you've left behind— well, I'm just glad you two are still operational. Since

NorAmAsian looks to have been created by dirty money, chiefly Russian Mafia money, then I'd say keep the heat up on that angle. But for the moment we know that Pinchinko has been shipping his contraband via Borneo. Can you get on your fax sometime in the next thirty minutes so I can send you the critical intel, flight coordinates, iron out logistics? I know that may be looking a giant leap beyond Manila..."

Bolan allowed a grim smile. "But you're keeping the faith."

"And then some."

The soldier asked Grimaldi the ETA to their base, then relayed the answer to Brognola.

"I haven't slept since this thing started, Striker. I still have more questions than answers, but I think they're coming in little by little the more you kick them in the ass. As for going into Russia, I've got all our key people here at the Farm putting together what you'll need on who in the Russian Mafia is involved with NorAmAsian. Not too hard to do. We're turning up names, businesses, addresses the more we delve into this Russian-NorAmAsian connection. Where it all ends...all I can do is send you a hearty good luck and keep the ball rolling on this end.

"One other thing. I've established through the CIA case officer in Moscow a contact for you. It's a little-known countersurveillance organization, sort of an intelligence agency inside an intelligence agency. They monitor any known terrorist activity inside Russia. I'll have more for you ASAP on that item."

"Working with unknowns on this has proved more harm than good."

"You're going to need help inside Russia."

"When we touch down, I'll get back to you."

Bolan signed off. He met Pinchinko's angry stare for a moment, then said, "In the next ten minutes you're going to tell me everything you know about your Russian pals, McBain and your dealings in Borneo."

The guy played stupid.

It wasn't more than five seconds later when Bolan made a believer out of Pinchinko as the Executioner wrapped a fist through his belt buckle, dragged him to the open doorway, then dangled him by his ankles, face toward the dark earth sweeping past them.

"Okay, okay!" Pinchinko screamed. "I'll tell you everything, everything!"

Bolan felt his lips crack in a grim smile, hauled the NorAmAsian president back inside and dumped him on the floor.

HE HAD NEVER BEEN kicked in the chest by a mule, but Petre Kuschka imagined he now knew what that felt like. It was most unpleasant, to say the least, but he was alive.

Somehow he struggled to his feet. Everything swirled, burned, rippled in brilliant and blinding light around him. He thought he would vomit but stifled the urge. The physical pain, the humiliating knowledge that he had again failed...

The bastard Americans had done it again.

Rage cleared out the cobwebs. He sucked in several deep breaths. Soaked in sweat, his lungs, starved of air, on fire, he took in the kill. Nothing moved; the stench of roasting flesh pierced his senses. Disgusted, he stripped off his turtleneck, removed the Kevlar vest and hurled it into the fire. He touched the ugly bruises on his chest, winced, cursed.

Kuschka briefly recalled his near win. The American was quick, moved like lightning. One second Kuschka had him nailed, the AK-47 jumping around in his fists.

The damn gunship. The damn brazenness and relentless, near insane desire of his enemies to track, kill them.

Now what to do? More of his men lay dead. Another call back to his superiors at the hotel? No.

Kuschka scanned the wreckage. There. Incredibly one of the vehicles had survived the attack. He went to the Mercedes, found the keys in the ignition. Maybe someone, one of the guests, in a drunken stupor, had left the keys behind. Whatever. Why question this one piece of good fortune?

His jet was secured on one of the three NorAm-Asian private airfields. He had to get there, he heard his foggy mind tell him, struggling to breathe where the bullets had slammed him full in the chest, feeling as if his lungs were now collapsing against the incredible knifing pain in his breastbone.

He would see the American again; he was sure of it, counted on it, in fact. They knew where the others were; they sat in the top-floor suite, rats in a barrel.

He didn't give a damn any longer about his superiors, about the Coalition. He had already lied to Turbov when first calling, saying that he would stay put. Instead he was right there in Manila, intent on showing up at the hotel. The act alone signaled Turbov that Kuschka knew his days were numbered. Pride was all he had left.

He would rather die than have to live any longer

with the knowledge that the two Americans were still
alive and kicking ass.

The Russian settled in behind the wheel of his getaway vehicle and fired up the engine. The rage, the
pain had become so unbearable that Kuschka wasn't
even aware he'd punched out the windshield until he
was driving away and a piece of glass blew back and
hit him in the face.

11

If it wasn't wrapped up in five minutes, give or take, they would either be dead or swarmed over by the Filipino police, either by ground or air. It was too late to look back; Bolan and Grimaldi were throwing everything they had at the enemy, not to mention tossing all caution to the high winds buffeting the New Hotel Manila.

While most of the city slept, the two warriors were locked in to finish up business in Manila. Their enemies, however, would hardly be nodding off.

With the sound suppressed mini-Uzi leading, Bolan cracked open the door to the service stairwell and peered down the long, carpeted, palm-tree-lined, wall-mirrored and seemingly empty hallway on the eighteenth floor. He listened for any sound of life. Nothing stirred. He checked the wall mirrors. No one opened doors along the hallway; no reflections of a lurking gunman.

So far, it looked as if the CIA intel—for whatever that was worth—combined with his grilling of Pinchinko, was holding. The Russian envoy had snagged up the eighteenth and nineteenth floors, apparently leaving them empty. Maybe weapons and important documents were stored in the suites on the vacant floors, or perhaps a security force was holed up behind the big double teak doors, midway down the hall, then again at the far end. There was no time to check it out. If anything was left over after the blitz, other authorities could step in, pick up the pieces, sort it out.

Bolan was going to assume the worst—bigger enemy numbers than reported, no good guys in white hats—and the only thing he was in search of was enemy blood. For the Manila finale, the Executioner was outfitted for all-out combat: M-16 with M-203 grenade launcher across his shoulder, standard side arms, spare clips all around, frag, incendiary and teargas bombs, both hand and 40 mm grenades for the M-203, with gas mask fixed to his webbing. The black war paint was gone, stealth pretty much tossed out of the equation. The enemy would be geared up and waiting, no doubt, given the fact the late Petre Kuschka was at the Pinchinko compound. While the enemy operation in Manila was burning down around them, they had dug in most likely, were cocked and locked.

No problem.

No way.

Review and assess. Pinchinko was cuffed to the bench in the Huey, to be dealt with again when Grimaldi evaced Bolan. Then they'd fly to one of three airfields owned by NorAmAsian, the two warriors intent on making the one airfield Pinchinko claimed was used only in emergencies, which meant, according to the NorAmAsian president, no ground personnel. Of course, Pinchinko could lead them into a small army of guns waiting for them at his airfield. But Bolan intended to contact the blacksuits at their own base, have them recon, secure the airfield. Even still an airborne force of Filipino authorities could chase them out to sea.

Again Bolan listened to the silence down the hall. It had been easy getting into the New Hotel Manila, with no front-lobby entrance, where the Russians had planted one of their own behind the desk. They'd flown in from the east, knowing the enemy was gathered on the twentieth floor, last suite, facing west toward the harbor. No lookouts had been posted on the roof, all security alleged to be with McBain.

After Grimaldi dropped off Bolan, he'd flown south, circling back, waiting for the soldier to raise him. Timing was everything, at least in the opening moments, where a lightning, coordinated ground and air assault should decimate most of the enemy.

The Executioner climbed the steps, used his lock pick to open the door to the nineteenth floor. The same stretch of silence and emptiness greeted the Executioner.

Cautious, Bolan swiftly went for the bank of elevators, hit the buttons for each of the three cars. Numbers began to flash from the lobby. At that late hour, when most of the guests were asleep, it would look suspicious to any sentries posted on twenty to see the lights coming their way. They would wait, guns poised for the cars to arrive. Of course the elevators weren't going all the way to the top.

But the Executioner was.

Bolan got on the handheld radio as he slipped back through the service door and raised Grimaldi.

IT WAS HAPPENING, and it was time to save himself.

They were scrambling beyond his door, shouting in Russian, bolts cocking on weapons. McBain was moving away from his bedroom window, as the powerful searchlight hit the curtains, then panned on. The whump-whump of rotors hovered right outside his window, a deafening noise that rocked the walls, vibrated the windows. Gunship.

And he imagined the Russian fools were massing at the living-room window that looked out to the harbor, or were near the curtained doors to the balcony.

They were dead meat.

McBain raced out into the living room. And indeed found them bunched, armed shadows behind the curtains, the finger of light washing over them, outlining them like stick figures, living bull's-eyes. And, like kids, he saw a few of them were even peeking through the curtains. He heard the shadow's voice barking in Russian, saw silhouettes scurrying around in the blue light. McBain then stared at the dark bulk of the gunship, hovering just beyond the floor-to-ceiling windows like some hideous predatory insect.

Then it all went to hell, just as he knew it would, just as he had seen in his dreams and in the horrifying reality of the longest week of his life.

But McBain was already dropping behind a pillar near the kitchen alcove. The thunderous noise was deafening. The pilot blew in the windows with his opening barrage of minigun fire. Bodies, McBain glimpsed, were sailing all over the living room, shredded, gutted to hell. The blue light sparked, fell, flickered, as if it were alive and gasping its last blue breath. The former general hugged his cover as glass, stone and blood flew around the place in a hurricane of wind.

Then, incredibly, the flyboy unloaded a rocket into the living room, or maybe it was two explosions.

McBain nearly kissed the pillar, riding out the explosion, thinking only of running like hell, glad he was still in one piece, breathing. While they died, he would run. But what about his money? It was somewhere, had to be in the dying blue light. The goddamn shadow probably clutched it even now.

McBain chanced a look around the pillar, saw a group of Russians running for the foyer, but for them he knew it was likewise too late. The big, ice-eyed nightmare would be there and waiting.

Then he saw it. Hope. First the discarded AK-47, stretching out before him, within easy reach, a cherished gift as the light from the gunship strobed around the room and the minigun kept rattling out death and dropping and flinging Russians all over the place. McBain hauled up the AK-47, then plucked a Makarov pistol off the bloody ruins of a Russian. He tucked the pistol in the small of his back, drew the bolt on the AK-47 as the walls were gouged by bullets and smeared by blood. Then he spotted his suitcase. Unbelievably it was still intact, bullets zipping past it by mere inches, laying there, right at the end of the table of the big shots.

It was now or never.

McBain dashed for the briefcase.

''McBain!''

Instantly he recognized the shadow's voice. He saw a grizzled, doughy face and bald dome loom into sight, directly across the room. Before his interrogator fired the first shot with his own AK-47, McBain stitched the Russian from crotch to sternum, blew him back into the sparking bed of his flickering blue lights.

McBain made his dive for his suitcase, unflinching,

as bullets kept tearing into the living, the dead and the dying.

THE FIRST PICKINGS were the easiest, but Bolan had expected as much.

He was cracking the door, counting eight black-garbed figures with AK-47s, staring up at the lights flashing above the elevators, when Grimaldi went to work in a sudden roar that Bolan felt shake the ground beneath his feet. From his southern point at the end of the hall, the soldier clearly heard all the racket of minigun fire, the explosion of a 2.75-inch rocket or two, and the piercing screams of men dying at the opposite end of the hall.

Bolan unloaded with his mini-Uzi, cutting them down as they spun away from the elevators and began a race to their CP suite. Crouched and holding back on the mini-Uzi's trigger, the Executioner zipped them up the backs, shattered skulls, flung them to the carpet.

Then the enemy opened the doors at the far end of the hallway.

Slinging the mini-Uzi across his shoulder, Bolan drew the M-16 and slipped a finger around the trigger of the M-203.

Five hardmen raced forward and five retreated into the suite on the tail end of the 40 mm grenade that blew with a deafening thunderclap and dismembered and shredded the enemy into oblivion.

Bolan donned his gas mask. It would obscure his vision some, but the tear gas was an added bonus to the blitz that would line them up, blind, in his gun sights. He reloaded the M-203 with a tear-gas grenade, moved out into the hall, then found his plans nearly shot to hell.

A door midway down the hall burst open, and AK-47s blazed, lead whining off the doorjamb behind Bolan, tracking, shattering a wall mirror beside him, his image tumbling around his feet in countless shards as he sprinted for cover behind a giant palm tree.

Popping around the trunk of the tree, Bolan loosed the tear gas on his unexpected target. Downrange it blew, spewing fumes in the doorway in a sizzling cloud. There was plenty of coughing and gagging, and the inevitable happened.

The Executioner was ready with his assault rifle, slid up closer to cover and swung the M-16's muzzle around the base.

Three black-clad hardmen staggered into the hallway, pinched faces, tearing eyes, mouths vented and bellowing in either agony or rage. Their Kalashnikovs roared for several heartbeats, their firing blind and wild.

Bolan dropped them with a neat line of rattling 5.56 mm death.

He loaded another gas bomb into the M-203's breech and sent it chugging down the hall, through the smoking maw of the suite's foyer. Sounds of autofire from somewhere in the suite were brief, then the expected gagging and hacking rent the air as tear gas sucked up oxygen and pierced lungs.

Just to make sure no enemy blundered out into the hall, Bolan armed a frag grenade and pitched it into the swirling smoke cloud. The hell-bomb blew; the hacking stopped.

Bolan hit the door, crouched, then looked inside.

Raising Grimaldi, he said, "I'm going into the living room. What's the bird's-eye view?"

"I'm still looking. I want to believe I nailed most of them with the first barrage, but keep your eyes peeled."

"I copy."

Everything smoked, sparked and hissed before Bolan. Gas and water swirled and sprayed the room, with the wind blowing through the shattered glass. He could see the gunship suspended beyond the long line of jagged window teeth, the city lights flickering beyond the chopper. Water kept hissing from overhead sprinklers; an alarm wailed.

Bolan charged inside, fanning his flanks with his assault rifle, then cut loose, on the fly, with his M-16, knocking two dark shadows off their feet down an adjacent hall.

Then Grimaldi ripped free with the minigun as several wounded figures staggered upright near the shattered windows. Glass blasted and bodies erupted, crimson sieves, puppets on a string, their AK-47s chattering toward the ceiling as the doomed hardmen spun and collapsed.

Rotor wash quickly dispersed the tear gas. Bolan listened, loosed another tear-gas grenade down one hallway to his flank, then reloaded and hit the hallway on his other side. Gas hissed, but there were no sounds of retching.

Glass crunched under Bolan's feet, as he scanned the carnage. Inside, the suite was immense, capable of containing the blasts from Grimaldi's rocket fire without razing the roof. Bodies twitched in pools of blood, or absorbed sparks flaying them from the ruins of computers and fax machines. Command post. Communicating with Borneo? Moscow?

Cold water sprayed Bolan's head as he moved deeper into the shadows of the living room. Grimaldi rotated the gunship, panned the searchlight around the slaughter.

Nothing stirred.

Over his handheld radio, Bolan told Grimaldi, "We're through here. Meet me up top. Two minutes and counting. What's the bird's-eye?"

"No sign of unfriendlies taking to the skies, but I've got plenty of flashing lights, north and east. The natives are pissed. Maybe five, six blocks away. Time to boogie, Striker."

"Roger that. On the way. Sit tight."

Grimaldi copied, then lifted off.

The Executioner stood as still as stone, combat senses tuned, electrified to any movement, any sound, among the carnage. He was scanning the devastation when he saw paper fluttering in the air from the far corner of the living room. The soldier moved forward and heard a soft whimpering sound. He whirled in the direction of the sobbing, finding a lumpy shadow crouched over the chewed remains of a briefcase.

The soldier dropped his gun sights on William McBain.

The former general was bleeding from the upper chest, on his knees, praying to the only god he worshiped. He seemed to be aware Bolan was looming nearby, but the man who had betrayed his country, his oath and duty, was only concerned with grabbing up stacks of hundred-dollar bills.

"You bastard," Bolan heard the man snarl.

McBain looked up, hatred in his stare. Money floated around his face.

"I'd rather take you alive than dead, McBain."

"Thirty years," the former five-star general cried. "All the wiretaps, the double-dealing, the surveillance, fuckers knowing I was dirty, only they end up protecting me, my own, our own!"

"Not sure who your own are, but you can believe I'm not one of them."

"Yeah, is that right? Who do you work for, then? You're American! You work for the same government I do!"

"I'd say the similarities end right there."

Bolan saw McBain stretch out a bloody hand for an AK-47. A short burst into the floor with his M-16, and Bolan discouraged any further attempt from McBain to grab up the weapon.

"All right, all right." McBain raised his hands, then stood. "I'll go with you. Peaceful. Lead me to the slaughter, all the stupid shits, the public that thinks it knows something about the world. You can throw me up before a bunch of numb-nut politicians on the Hill who know where the country and the world are headed but don't have the guts, the vision to make a stand."

"Is that what you think you're about? Saving America? The world? By destroying it and putting into place the ones you think deserve to live?"

"Only the strong will inherit the earth."

"I remember you told me that. I'm afraid you won't be one of the inheritors."

"No problem."

It was the look of murderous rage, then some flicker of despair in McBain's eyes that tipped Bolan off. The ex-general reached behind his back, hauled a pistol into Bolan's sight.

The Executioner squeezed the M-16's trigger, ending thirty years of McBain's dreams for good. Or maybe it was just misery.

12

Borneo

"I'm looking for Mick," the Executioner announced.

A razor-thin man with a gaunt face, sunken eyes and shoulder-length black hair looked up from behind the stacked wooden crates that passed as a bar. He studied Bolan with suspicion, then poured himself a shot of booze.

Two other men were in the longhouse, but Bolan was already told he would find the three wild Americans of Borneo here. A giant with tattoos of snakes, crocodiles and naked women writhing over his shaved skull stopped honing his knife on the stone long enough to glance up at their unexpected visitor, then returned to sharpening the fierce-looking blade. The third river rat was a beefy guy with a rug of matted black hair covering his torso, back and front. Right then Wolf-man was examining an old Thompson submachine gun over a bottle of whiskey and a cigar.

From what Bolan had gathered so far—by paying for information in a nearby fishing village, regarding where he could find someone to take him upriver— they were Vietnam vets. Presumably, he had learned in a bar, after loosening the tongue of a drunk American who knew his way around, they were listed as

MIA back in the States, but they had chosen to stay behind after the war, then somehow relocated to Borneo. Word was they dabbled in just about everything, from running tourists upriver to the jungle of Indonesian Borneo, to transporting guns, narcotics, whatever else paid. Bolan wasn't interested in anything more than a ride. Unless, of course, they were aiding his enemies. He was also looking to buy some information.

Glancing around, his eyes hidden by aviator shades, Bolan took in the room. It was hot as hell in there, sweat soaking into his green jungle camous, but he was looking to turn the heat up elsewhere and discomfort would soon be the least of his problems. His holstered Beretta didn't escape their observation. The soldier also carried a duffel bag, stuffed with maps, satellite photos, money and a mini-Uzi. Just in case the three wanted to do business the hard way.

The place wouldn't warm the hearts of any nature conservationists, Bolan observed. Tiger teeth and claws, as well as alligator carcasses, hung from the walls, along with mounted rhino and elephant heads. A couch and three recliners were lined in tiger skin. Other than the trophies, there was a radio console in one corner, a giant-screen TV, but Bolan had seen the satellite dish on his way in. The place assaulted the eyes first, the nose second. The men reeked of smoke and booze. They sweated profusely, slick with moisture, as if they'd just stepped out of the shower, even as two small fans hummed, blowing a hot breeze around the room. With the longhouse perched right on the river, raised on stilts, it sat away from any tree cover, and the blazing sun of early afternoon seemed to suck the air right out of the room.

It also didn't escape Bolan's scrutiny all three men wore pistols in shoulder holsters, and Mick and Wolfman had big knives sheathed on their hips. Assault rifles, submachine guns and shotguns leaned against the hardwood walls.

"Who the hell are you?" Mick growled.

"I'm someone with twenty thousand dollars to spend."

Bolan had their undivided attention but sensed he had aroused more than just their greed. "I want you to take me upriver about fifty miles. I've got a map in my pocket, and the course is already charted for you. I want you to rent my friend your twin-engine Cessna. We'll set up our own radio communications. And I'd like to leave within the hour."

"You want a lot for twenty grand."

"Ask no questions, I'll tell you no lies. When I get to where I'm going, I want you to drop me off and wait for my return. For this I'll pay you twenty thousand dollars, half now, half when I'm ready to leave."

"Three-way split of twenty grand leaves one of us short."

"I'm not here to bargain on hurt feelings. Take it or leave it."

It wasn't the most cordial of approaches, but Bolan didn't have time for tact or haggling over dollars. Calhoun was close, if he didn't miss his guess, and the soldier was running low on patience.

It had been roughly an eight-hour run from the blitz on the New Hotel Manila to the deserted airfield where Bolan and Grimaldi had fueled and commandeered one of Pinchinko's private jets. The sleek white bird, similar in design and specs to a Gulfstream-IIIA, complete with auxiliary tanks and a ferry range of close to six thousand miles, had then flown the three of them from Luzon to the world's third largest island, Borneo.

According to Stony Man Farm intel and satellite photos, a remote compound had been pinpointed in the jungle interior of the state of Kalimantan, up the Barito River, about sixty-two miles as the crow flew from where their jet had touched down on another remote airstrip. The airfield was previously found cleared of occupants by Stony Man, and was discovered abandoned when they had landed. According to Pinchinko, who often mixed business with pleasure in Borneo, the airfield was for his personal use, arrangements always made before he left Manila. This time, though, Pinchinko was a prisoner, sitting with Grimaldi who waited in a Land Rover they had taken at the airfield. Gifts from Pinchinko were turning up everywhere, but Bolan wasn't about to bet today on fateful accommodations.

Mick sucked down another shot. "Show me the money, as they say."

As Bolan zipped open his duffel bag, he noted a rattan net hanging beside the mounted head of a water buffalo. Stuffed with human heads, Bolan figured fifteen, maybe twenty pairs of dark eyes stared him back. "Is that decoration or mere ambience?"

Wolf-man grinned at the net of heads. "It's the real thing, pal. Dayaks. And it's for both. Also a message for the wrong person."

Nodding, Bolan withdrew a stack of bills, tossed it across the room where it landed on a crate next to Mick, who made a long show of counting the bills. The soldier waited.

"You're ten grand short."

"I've got the rest with me. Do we deal?"

Swiveling on his stool, Mick faced Bolan. "Let me see these maps."

Bolan walked across the room, pulled out his maps and satellite photos and set them on the crate next to Mick, who examined them. "These ain't your standard aerial photos or tour guides. Right. Almost forgot. Ask you no questions..."

"You're not CIA, are you?" Wolf-man asked. "We hate CIA. Got a spook head in that net, by the way."

"No. What I am is anxious to get upriver to this compound. What I'm willing to do is pay you an additional amount for some information."

"You're talking a lot and showing me little except a lot of attitude, friend," Mick said.

Bolan took another stack of bills and handed them over. "I believe you're giving me a yes."

"I believe you're a lot of bad fucking trouble, friend," Mick replied, riffling through the bills. "I'm sure you know who and what's up that river or you wouldn't be here, armed to the teeth and looking like you're ready to fight the world. What you don't know is that you're right now at the ass end of the planet, at the ass end of so-called civilization. People disappear in Borneo, never seen again, tourists, spooks, National Geographic types. Forget the rumors about stepping into the twenty-first century. They still take heads here. Hell, I've even seen them dropped into a Dayak pot and cooked. Ate the son of a bitch, right before my eyes. Part of a wedding ceremony, it was."

"I know exactly where I am."

"Do you now? Bobby," Mick said to the man with the tattooed skull. "Tell the man."

"Ebola."

Impatient, Bolan gritted his teeth as Bobby massaged his skull. "What?"

"Ebola. Ever hear of it?"

"It's fatal, nine times out of ten. It's a level-four virus, the worst there is. No cure. It's found in Africa, but it was reported discovered in test monkeys that were shipped from the Philippines to Reston, Virginia, a few years back. You want to get to it, and stop talking in riddles?"

"There're a whole bunch of guns up that river, pal," Bobby said. "We got Ivans. We got Chinese. Maybe North Koreans. They got covered racks, look like missiles under the tarps. They've got some kind of compound, guys running around in biohazard suits. Doing some kind of experiments, way we figure. An entire Dayak tribe was found nearly liquified by what appeared to be Ebola. I found them. Blood was still exploding from a few survivors, pouring out of every hole, the eyes, the ears, assholes, name it. Scared the hell out of me, and I know fear, I know death. Did three tours, and a level-four virus scares me more than a bullet with my name on it.

"This recon we did was two weeks ago. Since then the Dayaks upriver have gone on a rampage, killing their own, killing other tribesmen. Head-hunting is alive and well in Borneo. They're scared of evil spirits, you see. This virus is evil incarnate, killing them off, and they're hanging heads by the bushel, fifty miles up the river where you want to go. Let me tell you, I saw Ebola once in Zaire when I did some work for a now deposed dictator, and I'll never forget it. Whatever this thing is, well, it looks like it's ten times as hot as Ebola."

Bolan's mind tumbled with the horror, realizing he had stumbled onto a main enemy base where they were producing biological warfare. Was the enemy experimenting on the local Dayak tribes? It appeared so. Had the enemy infected themselves? Soon to find out. When the shooting started, was there a chance of virus-infected blood hitting Bolan, Grimaldi? To stop the enemy's nightmare agenda, it was worth the risk. The Executioner was no stranger to the ravaging effects of the Ebola virus. It had to be done.

"I flew back over the compound a few days ago," Wolf-man said. "They were burning dozens of bodies. Shot at the plane and put a few holes through the belly. Far as your friend or whoever you want flying my twin engine into this corner of hell, I would rethink that."

"I already am."

Mick was scouring the map. "Whoever they are, and word is they're mostly Russians, they've developed a new strain of Ebola and are either looking to use it on this state or export it, I don't know. I've seen spooks crawling all over this river lately. I don't know what it all means, but these bastards upriver have enough clout, firepower, money, whatever else, to buy up that piece of real estate and be left alone. They're dangerous and they need to leave Borneo, like yesterday."

"That's why I'm here."

"It's thirty grand, altogether," Mick declared.

"You realize I could try somewhere else?"

"You could," Mick said. "Then again, you wouldn't be able to find your own three wild men who were willing to go into this compound with you and blow these bastards off the island."

Bolan didn't know the enemy numbers, whatever else he might be faced with. To take allies, unknown factors again, made sense, in a twisted way. Again it was a roll of the dice. They could turn on him, but Bolan decided to risk it.

"I know," Wolf-man said, "can you trust us?"

"I'm here already."

"You want the help or not?"

Bolan looked at the three men, then nodded. "I make the plan, I give the orders."

"You're paying—that's fair enough," Mick said.

THEY WERE WEAPONLESS, full of rage and fear, ready to burst with violence.

Calhoun read it in the eyes of what remained of his force.

The former Special Forces major was having to stress-check himself. He was sick of the jungle, scared of the biohazard suits patrolling the compound beyond the open windows of their thatched roof hut, terrified of the burning bodies. He knew very little about this aspect of the Coalition's plan, but he knew enough about Ebola to recognize the symptoms. The blood pouring from the eyes, the black vomit spewing from mouths. The shrieks of men dying an agonizing death as their brains fried with fever and their innards liquified and poured in black rivers out every opening.

"What are we going to do, Major?"

Calhoun was looking out at the compound, the motor pool of Land Rovers and military-style jeeps, the generator, the twin-engine planes and helicopters sitting on the runway that had been slashed into the jungle, mind racing for some alternative to sitting on their hands. Three men in biohazard suits then walked with a dozen Russians wielding AK-47s near the edge of the jungle tree line. They disappeared into a hut. A moment later autofire rang out. More dead Dayaks, infected with Ebola. Or was it even Ebola? he wondered.

Turning, Calhoun stared with what he hoped was resolve at Pumpton. The rest of his men were pacing around the hut, all lean and mean, bearded, drenched in sweat, ready for a fight.

"Our Ivan comrades are holding us prisoners—you know that, don't you, Major?" Wellington stated.

"It's a frigging horror show out there, sir. I say we make a break. Grab a plane, chopper, whatever and forget this whole insane deal."

Barker. The man was sweating so much in the stifling heat, his shoulder-length hair looked like someone had just dumped a bucket of water on his head.

"That would be most unwise."

Calhoun couldn't believe his eyes at first. Kuschka had appeared in the doorway, flanked by two former Spetsnaz commandos, as silent as wraiths. It was the look of hatred, coupled with the smell of fear and defeat on the Russian killer, that Calhoun noted right off.

"Back from Manila? Problems, Comrade?" Calhoun asked bitterly.

Kuschka barked an order over his shoulder. Three more commandos hurried into the hut and they began to toss AK-47s to Calhoun's men. When Calhoun caught his own assault rifle, he checked the clip, found it full, cracked it home, then racked the bolt. He resisted the fleeting urge to cut loose, spray bullets, drop Kuschka, make that final run for it.

"Our hunters," Kuschka stated, "have struck

again. Our operation in Manila has been compromised. Arm yourselves, prepare to fight to the last man, for I know our adversaries will come.''

Calhoun suppressed his murderous feelings toward Kuschka. Time and again their nemesis had kicked him and his men in the teeth. He had lost many good soldiers since New York, not to mention lost face. Let alone his confidence in his ability to lead, to fight.

It was time, though, to find a way to save himself and his surviving soldiers. Their adversary would show—again. How and when, he didn't know.

For the moment it was enough that Calhoun was back on board. When the shooting started, and he knew it would, he would find a way out. Run like hell. There was always some mogul, dictator, drug lord out there who would pay for his services. He could recoup the loss of his own invested money in due time. First and last Calhoun meant to save his own skin, to live to fight and get paid another day.

''What the hell's going on here, Kuschka?'' Calhoun heard a shrill cry of mindless agony beyond the hut, followed by the stutter of autofire. ''Are we in danger of catching what's killing those Dayaks?''

''No, the only danger we face is two nameless pains in our asses. And what's going on?'' Kuschka paused, squared his shoulders. ''What's going on is quite possibly the beginning of the end of the world.''

The sixty-foot gunboat sluiced up the calm olive waters of the Barito River. Sitting on a bench, amidships, Bolan pored over the maps of the jungle interior surrounding the target compound.

As the diesel engines throbbed and they moved along at twenty knots, the sun burning into the deck, Bolan mentally put together a plan of attack. It would be a standard silent penetration, moving in on foot, five heavily armed men against six, with seven times that many enemy numbers, according to the river rats. They would go in from the south, eyes peeled for booby traps, cameras, motion sensors, sentries. But Bolan figured the enemy would stick close to the compound, not go tramping through the jungle on patrol or laying out mines along the trails. The jungle was always deadly enough during daylight—at night it could be a sure killer. Thus they'd launch a strike before nightfall. Either way, he would take it as it came. The enemy should be on high alert. It stood to reason this force of the Coalition had been informed of the decimation of their comrades in Manila, and Bolan was taking nothing for granted.

The compound was roughly a mile-and-a-half hike through the jungle. Once there, they'd throw everything they had at the enemy, in a pincer attack, in sync down to the second. If the enemy came to them during their penetration, well, it was a situation Bolan had dealt with countless times before.

The Executioner glanced across the deck where Grimaldi sat beside Pinchinko, who was cuffed and glaring back at Bolan. The Stony Man warriors had their M-16s with attached M-203 grenade launchers, side arms, combat knives, grenades, clips all around, while Bolan would also carry with him ten pounds of C-4 plastique and a radio activator. Toward the stern of the gunboat, near the mounted .50-caliber machine gun, Bobby and Wolf-man were going over their own armament. Strangely enough they had said nothing so far about Pinchinko. He had been glanced at, then ignored.

And Bolan saw his mercenary volunteers were serious about getting the job done so they could spend his thirty grand. An M-60 machine gun had been belted with 7.62 mm slugs and bandoliers of the NATO bullets were strung out over the deck, looked over by Tattoo, who was certainly big and strong enough to wield the heavy weapon in combat. Two Israeli Galil assault rifles were checked by Wolf-man. Then Bobby and Wolf-man began to fix grenades to their webbing. There were also three LAW rockets to give their side extra punch, and each of his three mercs, he suspected, would carry a launcher. Whatever else they were, Bolan read the river rats as fighting men, mercenaries, modern-day pirates, to be sure, but he sensed he could count on them when it hit the fan. Soon he would lay out the strategy. Bobby and Wolf-man would go with Grimaldi. If Mick read some distrust on Bolan's part by splitting up the three of them, then so be it. He figured Mick would understand, go with the program.

The river widened thirty minutes later, and what looked like the last of civilization, a lone longhouse on raised stilts, swept by Bolan's view. No river traffic flowed from the north for as far as he could see, the last of the brightly colored schooners, barges of timber, rafts, tour boats miles south now. A green and impenetrable forest loomed on both sides of the river.

Already the sun was beginning to set beyond the distant green lumps of hills to the west. Bolan intended to be at and on target well before nightfall, and figured he had maybe four hours to get there, get in, burn them down and get out. In case darkness descended and unforeseen circumstances impeded their march, Bolan and Grimaldi had NVD goggles. It turned out Mick likewise had several pairs of night-vision headgear at his disposal. Bolan wasn't surprised. He could only imagine what these guys had done in their lives, places they had gone, whom they killed and for whom or how much, whom they had maybe stepped on, cheated, betrayed. Any hint of betrayal and Bolan would gun them down without blinking.

Mick stepped from the wheelhouse, obviously having put the boat on autopilot. He nodded at Pinchinko, asked Bolan, "What about that one, Captain? I take it you two ain't drinking buddies."

"He stays behind. Someplace to stow him?"

"Cargo hold, stern."

"I want him gagged, feet tied and tossed in there. Make sure he can get some air."

"And what am I to do while the rest of you go

traipsing off through the jungle to most likely get killed? I will be trapped without food and water.''

"If we get killed," Bolan told Pinchinko, "your worries are over. Toss him."

Mick gave Bobby the order. The big man took a rag, stuffed it in Pinchinko's mouth, then trussed up his legs with rope. "This is going to hurt you a lot more than me," Bobby said, then banged a right off Pinchinko's jaw, laid him out cold and dragged the limp form to the cargo hold, dumped him down the hole.

"Guess now we can talk," Mick said. "First I don't know who your girlfriend is, but your problem could become ours, if you catch my drift. If you don't make it back, what am I supposed to do with him? Toss him overboard to the crocs? Cut him loose at the local watering hole, buy him a round, have a nice day? Ain't happening. That guy is somebody, the fancy silk threads, cocksure air of money and self-importance. Who and what he is, I don't know, don't care. But what if he has a long memory and a lot of bad friends?''

"I'll make it back to deal with him."

"You seem pretty sure of yourself. Okay. Fair enough, to a point. I read you as one tough nut, dodged more than a few bullets, kicked some major ass along the way. But a future bullet doesn't play favorites with past heroics."

"I'm aware of that."

"Are you now. So?"

"Turn him loose, warn him to not return, tell him you don't know a damn thing about him and his dealings with us. Whatever you have to do. Can you do that?''

"Throw another three grand into the pot, and you've got an affirmative, Captain."

Bolan reached into his duffel and handed over the money. "You're wearing my money and my patience thin. Enough said on the matter?"

"Never hear about it again, Captain."

True, if they were all killed, then Pinchinko was on his own, tossed to fate. Bolan was no sadist, but he had no choice but leave Pinchinko behind, stowed away. The Filipino could find his own way back if none of them returned. Food and water would be left behind, and Bolan would see to it the cargo hold was left open so the man could breathe. All along Pinchinko had been a prime target, and the soldier had needed him at arm's reach up to then in case the man sounded the alarm and set a force of hardmen on his tail or alerted key enemy players beyond Luzon. Now that his operation was rooted out for the whole world to see what NorAmAsian was—a criminal enterprise—it was only a matter of time before Hal Brognola put the wheels of justice in motion to dismantle the corporation.

Even though he put Pinchinko out of mind, Bolan's attentions toward NorAmAsian were far from over. Provided they crushed the enemy agenda in Borneo, the soldier knew Brognola was already hard at work paving the way for an excursion into the new, improved and democratic Russia.

The Executioner, indeed, had a date to keep with the Russian Mafia.

"Here's what I suggest, Captain," Mick said. "I got us a place I can anchor. Right off a tributary that runs up close to the compound like I told you. I've got a raft, big enough to hold all of us and our gear, but I suggest we paddle in close as we can. No engine noise to alert any restless natives other than a few wandering Dayaks.''

"That sounds wise.''

"During your flyover,'' Grimaldi asked Wolf-man, "how many guns you figure we're facing?''

"Hard to say. I climbed soon as they started shooting. Rough guess is thirty, forty.''

"Can you give us a rough idea of what you saw?'' Bolan asked.

"You've got a runway, east of the compound. Big cargo planes, two of them, Russian Antonovs. You've got three choppers, three twin-engine planes. Maybe six thatched-roof huts for the troops or the guinea pigs or whoever they're experimenting on.''

"Not bad for a quick flyover while being shot at,'' Grimaldi commented.

"So call me Hawkeye. Anyway, they also got a giant sat dish, huge fuel bins, the way I read it, maybe twenty, hell, thirty thousand gallons could be in those whales. Motor pool, maybe a dozen vehicles. Body pit, where they dump the dead, or the infected. Outer west perimeter. You can't miss it, if they're burning bodies, and I got to imagine the smell in this heat will knock you off your boots. One long structure, at the west edge, near the jungle tree line, metal. Probably their CP.''

"Or laboratory,'' Bolan said. "Which brings me to a rather unnerving point. Infectious blood. If it looks like a hot zone, laboratory, biohazard suits, vials, test tubes, decon bins, stay away. Same thing with any native hostages. Focus on taking out the gunmen. Keep your distance from whoever looks sick or dying.''

"Oh, you'll know them if you see them," Bobby said. "On this I prefer long-distance work, like at about a thousand yards, but, hey, they say only the good die young and I ain't so young no more. Even with that, I still don't savor the idea of going toe-to-toe with some asshole bursting with viral-laden blood. If it's native Dayak, they're on their own. Let some Red Cross diaper team or Christian missionaries come in here to tend to the sick and dying."

"What if this disease is airborne?"

Grimaldi had a good point, Bolan knew. "I don't think so, but we don't know. We don't have biohazard suits, but from what I hear, the troops aren't wearing them, which indicates it probably isn't airborne. If possible," the soldier told them, "I want one of the guys wearing biohazard suits taken alive for questioning. In other words, try not to kill indiscriminately. What's the ETA on anchor time?"

"Maybe another fifty minutes at the outside, Captain."

"Okay, I've been looking at the area east of the compound, upstream. These hills, east along the runway, and here's where my fuel bins are," Bolan said, stabbing the map with his finger.

"Already saw the plastique, Captain," Mick said, grinning. "Sounds like you've got your own ideas on slash and burn."

"Well, then, here's the game plan," the Executioner announced.

BOLAN CHANGED the game plan with some last-second improvising. The gunboat anchored near shore, they paddled east up the narrow tributary. It was risky, five men exposed in the raft, slugging

along the brown waters, paddling right past the point
of where they were originally going in.

The soldier listened, watched the wall of trees
along the shoreline. The jungle howled and shrieked
with monkeys, birds, the incessant buzz and whine of
insects. They sweated and paddled on as quietly as
possible, vigilance trained on the lush vegetation
along the banks.

On the south bank Bolan spotted three, then four
naked brown figures watching them—Dayak tribesmen, headhunters. And he saw their blowguns.

They paddled on without incident, and the dark figures melted back into the jungle.

Bolan wanted to off-load his crew at a point just
east of the compound, upstream, where the tributary
forked. There, the slash-and-burn tactics of modern
civilization shown on the satellite photos would allow
easier penetration, even though there was a greater
risk of being seen when they crept beyond the jungle.
But if they could be seen, so, too, could they spot
their enemies.

A series of hills lay east of the compound, and that
would be Bolan's point of penetration. If he could
circle the compound from behind the hills, come up
on the fuel bins, attach the C-4 to selected aircraft,
ignite the fuel and create wholesale panic and hopefully mass slaughter in the opening moments it would
shave the odds in their favor.

Bolan indicated a marshy strip of bank, where
some giant hardwoods had tumbled and would conceal their raft. By paddling farther upstream, Bolan
figured they had cut the gap to the enemy compound
by half. Timing was everything, as darkness was com-

ing fast and hard. Already long shadows were stretching over the brown waters.

They landed and off-loaded. Bolan pointed at his watch. Sixty minutes and counting, they knew, once they hit the shore.

They slithered onto a narrow trail. It was impossible, Bolan knew, to remain one hundred percent silent and invisible in any jungle. Leaves, vines, brush tore at a person. Primates would watch from the limbs above, or snakes would slither through the foliage, watching your every move.

Even still the ceaseless hooting of monkeys and the buzz of insects masked whatever noise they made. Would it be enough?

Finally, in the distance, through a break in the wall of trees and vegetation, Bolan saw the compound. He nodded at Grimaldi.

It was the cue to split up.

THEY MADE the far north edge of the runway with ten minutes to spare. So far, so good. And Bolan noted the intel he had received was pretty much on the money.

With Mick crouched in the brush beside him, Bolan gave the compound another hard search. During their run over the hills to the east, the soldier had counted maybe forty gunmen scattered around the compound, but pretty much bulked in the center of the complex, near the metal structure. No biohazard suits were in sight, but the air was tainted with the smell of blood and burned flesh. There was disease here, plenty of dead and dying, and Bolan had seen the body pit, at the far edge of the compound to the west. Even then there was a raging fire, consuming whoever had died of whatever diseases the enemy had created. If the virus his enemies had designed to unleash on the world went beyond the jungle of Borneo, Bolan knew he was glimpsing a mere flash of hell on earth.

It was the two hardmen, AK-47s slung across their shoulders, who took Bolan's immediate attention. They were standing guard near the stern of the closest Antonov. As he had been informed, aircraft lined the makeshift runway—twin engines, choppers, the two Russian cargo planes. In the distance, beyond the line of huts, Bolan heard voices talking in Russian. He also saw the tarps over the tracked carriers, which held missiles, no doubt.

If the bulk of the enemy here played true to form, a sudden lightning blow would result in a chaotic fighting withdrawal—the Russians would head for aircraft, ground transport, looking to bolt to fight another day. Then again maybe not, perhaps they were under standing orders to fight to the last man.

Experience told Bolan that during the chaos of battle, all bets were off. It could come down to every man for himself. Many of the enemy gunners would protect their only means out of the jungle, if it looked as if they would be thrashed. So Grimaldi and his fire team were geared up to send them charging into the guns of Bolan and Mick, near the motor pool and the runway. With the C-4 planted, Bolan hoped to catch them in a final fireball that would instantly scramble their numbers to near zero.

The compound was everything he had been told, and then some. The fuel bins were indeed behemoths, long hoses running from the bellies. They would provide the fiery touch they needed.

Other than the two sentries by the Antonov, Bolan

found no other gunmen around the runway. Time to
go to work.

Grimaldi and his two-man fire team were in position, to the west, counting down the doomsday
numbers.

Bolan checked his watch, then indicated to Mick
they take out the two sentries with their backs to
them. The Executioner drew his Ka-bar fighting knife
while Mick pulled his own large blade.

They stood twenty feet from the sentries, one of
whom fired up a cigarette. Twenty feet could be a
lifetime.

Bolan and Mick moved out, closing rapidly on the
sentries. It was quick and ugly—hands clamped over
their mouths, blades driving up through ribs, piercing
the heart. They eased the corpses to the ground,
pushed them under the Antonov's belly, then wiped
and sheathed their blades.

Bolan gave the runway a long search. In the distance a group of six gunmen emerged from a hut.
They glanced around, as if sensing something was
wrong, then disappeared to the west, behind the huts.

The Executioner went to work with the C-4, which
was already divided into two-pound blocks, with detonators inserted in all five blocks, to be detonated by
one radio frequency. He indicated for Mick to watch
his back, then the soldier moved out.

The first block went under the belly of the Antonov, starboard, near the wing. Then Bolan darted
across a short stretch of no-man's-land, alert for
guards, and set two more blocks, one to the wing of
a twin-engine plane, one beneath the front fender of
a Land Rover. The motor pool consisted of a dozen
vehicles, and the soldier selected the Land Rover that

was right in the middle. The vehicles were packed tight. One explosion should trigger a chain reaction once gas was flying and fire was eating up the other vehicles.

Four minutes and counting.

Now for the big ones.

He backtracked for the fuel bins and affixed the rest of the C-4. Then he twisted the valves, releasing fuel, lines of flammable liquid gushing out the hoses, rolling for the runway.

The soldier needed to put some quick distance between him and the spreading lake of fuel before he started the fireworks, but he never got the chance.

It went to hell in the next instant.

As Bolan slid away from the fuel bins, he spotted a trio of gunmen surging past the motor pool, shouting a warning across the compound, their AK-47 assault rifles already blazing. Then, from somewhere to the west, the rattle of autofire struck the air.

The Executioner dived to one side as bullets drilled into the fuel bin.

14

The soldier couldn't help but briefly wonder what had happened to tip off their enemies.

It was too late to curse misfortune; the alarm was sounded.

Bolan hit the ground on the fly, his face plastered into soft dirt for an eternal heartbeat, as the line of 7.62 mm slugs kept thudding into and whining off the fuel bin, and several whispering bullets zipped over the back of his skull, so close they parted hair and released a trickle of blood. A fraction of an inch closer to target, and Bolan would have had his brains spattered into the jungle foliage. Call it luck or fate, but some twist of good fortune had momentarily prevailed. Unloading ten pounds of C-4, which made Bolan considerably lighter on his feet, was what saved him.

That, and Mick hitting the trio of hardmen from their blind side.

The Executioner rolled up behind a line of fifty-five-gallon drums, popped up from cover to loose a burst from his M-16, but found AK-47s chattering wild fire at the sky. From beneath the wing of the Antonov, Mick hosed the enemy with his Galil until the trio finally pitched in crimson tatters and the guns stopped barking. He glimpsed a distinctly Asian face among the dead, maybe Korean. So, just like it had all begun on Long Island, they were again facing a mixed bag of hardmen.

The stench of fuel pierced Bolan's senses. He'd gotten lucky. One spark off the steel bin from a wild round, and he and Mick would have been blown back to the river. Adrenaline overdrive got Bolan going again.

"Come on, shake a leg!"

Mick didn't have to be told twice. Hefting the LAW around his shoulder, the merc made a break for Bolan, who provided cover while his ally bolted from the Antonov.

The game plan was to use the jungle, parallel the action from the enemy's rear, drive them, with help from Grimaldi and company, to the runway.

There and then, they'd unload the superbang.

It didn't matter if the fuel bins gushed out their last gallon of flammable liquid. A lake of fuel was now spreading beneath half the aircraft and surging on, flooding under the motor pool. In the chaos and confusion of the fighting, the enemy might not smell the gasoline until the trap was sprung. Once the C-4 blew, it would ignite a firestorm that would consume everything out on the runway, man and machine.

Provided, of course, it all got that far and Bolan was still breathing.

Linked up, the two men charged into the jungle, forging deep and hard to the west, angling for the compound. West, Bolan heard the endless and furious racket of autofire, the shrill cries of men dying in agony, then a series of explosions rocked the air.

Us or them, Bolan wondered, with the upper hand?

He would know soon enough.

IF IT WASN'T for Bobby, Grimaldi knew the three of them would have been dropped, dead before it even started. Maybe it was the guy's bizarre collage of artwork on his skull, allowing him to melt to near invisibility into the jungle foliage and bright array of flowers, just part of the scenery. Maybe it was just one of those crazy quirks of oversight on the enemy's part, or adrenaline and fear taking over, blinding them to all else, not seeing the real threat until it was too late.

Whatever it was, Bobby had risen from the orchids and the green brush like a silent wraith, opting for his huge blade and nearly decapitating both hardmen as they had lifted their weapons to hit Grimaldi and Wolf-man from their blind side.

Unfortunately nearly headless bodies still had nerve endings working in death spasms on fingers tightened around triggers.

All that seemed a lifetime ago now.

Right then Grimaldi and company were in for the fight of their lives.

The compound was a hornet's nest of mad activity. Thirty or forty hardmen raced all over the complex, shouting at one another, pointing west, then unleashing a storm of AK autofire. Then more enemy numbers seemed to multiply out of nowhere before Grimaldi's eyes. Gunmen hit crouches by the doorways of huts or streamed past the giant satellite dish, firing on the run. A truck engine gunned to life at the eastern edge of the compound, chugged ahead, hauling one of several tracked carriers.

Grimaldi sent a 40 mm grenade belching from his M-203, choosing a group of what looked to be Koreans near a large thatched-roof hut, twenty yards or so downrange to his right flank. He scored big the first time out, the fireball ripping their numbers to shreds, scattering body parts in all directions.

General panic took over, as the enemy scrambled, pell-mell, all over the compound, still darting out of huts, looking dazed and confused for the most part. And from what Grimaldi next observed, as more gunmen disgorged from the huts and from the jungle to the south, their river mercs looked off by twenty or thirty guns from their aerial recon.

As planned, Wolf-man and Bobby broke from his flanks for cover beside a thatched-roof hut on each side of him. Grimaldi held back on the trigger of his M-16, sweeping a line of 5.56 mm tumblers, left to right. He scored three kills, but by then the enemy had pulled it back together, returning fire with all the fear and fury of cornered animals. Foliage, brush and bark were chewed up around Grimaldi, but most of those shots were wide, loosed by dead or dying men.

Grimaldi's allies were hard at work.

Wolf-man pitched one frag grenade after another into the compound, while Bobby, howling in some berserker rage, charged ahead. The M-60 machine gun looked like a child's toy in the merc's massive fists. Shells twirled around his kaleidoscopic shaved head. The rattling streams of 7.62 mm slugs chopped down enough enemy numbers in the opening moments and, coupled with maybe four frag bombs scything them down, gave the fire team an epic body count already.

Even still, it was far from over.

Grimaldi had his sights set on a tracked carrier, dead ahead, to be used for concealment and his next firepoint. He saw the enemy breaking down the complex, in a herdlike backward shuffle for the runway, when a group of gunmen burst into what Grimaldi believed was either the command post or the laboratory. Shrill cries added more noise to the din of weapons fire outside. Then from inside the big metal structure, controlled bursts of autofire echoed and began silencing those shrill pleas. Obviously the hardforce had been ordered to execute whoever was in there. And who were the doomed? Grimaldi wondered. Dayaks? Scientists? Virologists?

Grimaldi knew the innocent, as well as the guilty, were on their own. All he could do was kill the guilty.

Breaking cover of the jungle, the ace pilot nearly froze in midstride when he saw a tall scar-faced figure rolling from around a hut near the end of the complex.

Kuschka.

How? Grimaldi wondered as he crouched behind the tracked carrier and bullets gouged up divots beside him. Bolan had informed him that he had dropped the former KGB assassin at Pinchinko's compound, and the Executioner wasn't one to give a false report on enemy kills or see what he wished to see. Never mind, Grimaldi told himself. Kuschka was alive and screaming out orders, holding both an AK-47 and an RPG-7 rocket launcher.

Then Grimaldi spotted Ben Calhoun's familiar face in the distance. The American contingent of the opposition was surging from the direction of the jungle tree line to the south. They appeared to be whittled down to maybe six, seven guns.

From inside the main building, the screams for mercy and the stutter of autofire went on and on. Grimaldi heard voices from that direction, shouting frantically in different tongues.

A return firestorm washed over the Stony Man pilot's position.

Chased to cover, Grimaldi loaded the M-203's breech. He chanced a peek, low around the treads of the carrier. The grenades blowing up and down the middle of the complex, and Bobby's M-60 pounding down the enemy, might have provided the immediate turning point where the enemy again decided a savage fighting withdrawal was in order. It was understandable in some respects. Time and again the enemy had been smashed, as the Stony Man warriors seemed to just drop from the sky or rise from the ground and all but kick their quarry to the edge of the grave. If there were still other horizons beyond Borneo, then the enemy might decide it best to abandon the game here, regroup.

They could regroup in hell, Grimaldi decided, and began to pick out targets. Beyond the shattered bodies, the wall of drifting smoke, Kuschka and Calhoun appeared shielded inside a human wall of their comrades. The two men and an Asian gunman alternated between screaming at one another and firing at the jungle. On the fly, Grimaldi held back on the M-16's trigger.

Bobby surged ahead, the M-60 roaring on and spraying the phalanx of gunmen, cutting through flesh, with Kuschka and Calhoun ducking and folding deeper inside the human wall.

Three or four hardmen spun and dropped under Grimaldi's blazing M-16, but the AK-47s in the hands of the other hardmen kept stuttering, raking the edge of the jungle, hosing the ground behind Grimaldi.

Then, several things took place within a few seconds, threatening to fling it back for good in Grimaldi's face.

Bobby bellowed in pain. Grimaldi checked his flank and glimpsed the giant dropping to one knee. Even as the blood spurted from his upper chest, Bobby kept firing the M-60.

Beyond the retreating enemy, Grimaldi saw the cab of the fleeing truck explode, while several groups of five to ten gunmen raced for the runway.

Then the goons who had gone into the metal building reemerged and began to fire at the Stony Man pilot for all they were worth. From behind the far edge of the building, Wolf-man lobbed a grenade toward the doorway.

Bullets tracked Grimaldi, who was running for his life.

The grenade blew, and an explosion tore through the rear of the enemy pack. Something then streaked from the bulk of the hardforce, heading Grimaldi's way even as bodies tumbled from the blast.

"Get down!" Grimaldi shouted, leaping from his feet and slamming into the earth behind a now tumbling Wolf-man as the RPG warhead hammered into the face of the metal building.

Before he knew it, wreckage and rubble pounded their position, and Grimaldi felt something bang off his head. He saw the ground rush to his face, hazy and spinning before he tasted dirt.

BOLAN AND MICK SURGED UP on the compound, coming in from the north. The soldier was unmindful of the blood running down his neck, the vines and brush tearing at his fatigues. Discomfort was acceptable; death for his allies or himself was not.

From the sounds of the fighting coming from the west, the screaming, the blasts of grenades, the ceaseless autofire, Bolan knew Grimaldi and company were still in the foray, but it also sounded as if they were under extreme return fire.

As Bolan had hoped, the enemy was making a break for the runway. From somewhere beyond the huts ahead, Bolan heard a voice shouting orders, a mixed garble of English and Russian. The voice sounded vaguely familiar, but it was hard to tell with all the sound and fury of all-out war.

Teams of gunners kept charging the aircraft, a few hardmen hopping into trucks and firing up engines. A truck pulling a missile carrier suddenly went up in a ball of flames. Bolan glanced at Mick, who tossed away the smoking and spent LAW rocket launcher.

It appeared the recon of the enemy numbers by his river mercs was off by at least thirty, maybe forty guns. Not that it mattered. From what he glimpsed of the carnage strewed around the compound, the hardforce was cut by half, at least, and they were retreating.

Bolan and his ally bolted ahead, then secured cover behind some hardwoods. After a short, hard run they perched at the back edge of two huts still intact, directly across from each other.

Bolan spotted the bulk of the retreating army as it came into sight, backing up between the two huts. The gunners were firing their weapons on their way to the runway, westward, oblivious to the threat on their flank. They didn't know what hit them at first, as Bolan unleashed a 40 mm grenade into the rear end of the pack. He aimed purposely at the rear, having glimpsed an RPG-7 team kneeling and drawing target acquisition on what he knew were his allies to the west.

The Executioner hoped he saved Grimaldi and company from a direct hit even as he scored his own bull's-eye with the 40 mm hellbomb. Missiles still whooshed on, bodies cartwheeling through the smoky air, but their aim was slightly thrown off, or so Bolan hoped.

Out of the corner of his eye, the Executioner saw the front of the main building erupt in a cloud of fire and smoke. If Grimaldi and company had been holding position from that direction...

Bolan shoved pessimistic thoughts out of mind.

As the soldier rammed a fresh 30-round magazine into his assault rifle, he saw a scarred face—and stared him right in the eye through a drifting pall of smoke.

Bolan felt his blood run cold. He was already squeezing the trigger of his M-16, going for a head shot on Kuschka, when two Asian gunmen stumbled across the tracking line of fire. As they absorbed lead meant for Bolan's prime target, the Russian and another line of shielding gunmen vanished beyond his position. The soldier ran behind the hut, prepared to greet his enemies. He whipped around the corner, spraying autofire, caught two Asian gunmen in the chest with a quick M-16 burst and flung them back. He found Mick crouched at the edge of the hut on his flank, turning loose his Galil, the merc's burst of 5.56 mm lead rewarded by sharp cries of pain.

Then, in the scuffle of men running for their lives, from beyond the swirl of smoke and cordite, Bolan met the angry gaze of Ben Calhoun. Again several gunmen surged between the former major and the soldier's intended line of fire.

Intended, hell.

Bolan let them have it just the same. He kicked three hardmen to the earth, saw the blood spray Calhoun, but the ex–Special Forces major was already pouring it on with his AK-47.

A swarm of bullets drove Bolan to cover. Lead drilled divots in the earth, lopped off hunks of wood by Bolan's head for long moments, Calhoun screaming and cursing at the top of his lungs.

The Executioner heard more engines growl to life, heard the turbofan whine of Antonovs gearing up to taxi down the runway.

The big American pulled the transmitter from a pouch.

Out on the runway he saw two gunmen slip in the pooling fuel. Propellors, rotors were spinning to life on the smaller aircraft, and armed hardmen were jumping into the bellies of the big birds.

Bolan then spotted Kuschka, standing tall, utterly still for some reason near the motor pool. The ex-KGB assassin began to shout at several men near him, then grabbed Calhoun by the shoulder and ran like hell. The prime targets were bolting out of Bolan's gun sights, sprinting behind one of the huts when Bolan activated the box with a flip of the switch and armed the detonators.

The Executioner figured at least three-quarters of the surviving enemy force was cranking up the escape vehicles. One Antonov was already rolling south.

Kuschka had figured it out, perhaps, but in a few seconds it wouldn't matter. If the ex-KGB assassin and Calhoun even survived what was coming, Bolan would chase them into the jungle and hunt them down.

Bolan thumbed the lone button on the transmitter box.

15

If they were scrambling around the runway, warming up the aircraft or trying to rev engines for escape by motor vehicle, they were finished.

Done deal, nothing left but the screaming.

At first there was a blinding flash, and the earth shook as if it were being cleaved open from deep in its bowels, then one long rumble of thunder hit the sky. The fuel bins went first, likewise the rolling Antonov obliterated as the C-4 blast blew out its belly, sheared off its wing and fire blazed back over the big transport bird when spewing fuel caught. A secondary fireball reduced it to fiery scrap.

Even from one hundred yards or so out from ground zero, the heat was so intense Bolan felt his face scorched, as if he'd just stuck his head in a broiling oven.

Elsewhere man and machine took to the air from the motor pool as the Land Rover went up in a ball of flames and the lake of fuel from that direction ignited, going off like the spray of dragon's fire.

It was only the beginning.

The fireballs erupted up and down the runway, sucking up everything with superheated gale-force wind, shredding and hurling everything in their blazing paths on all points of the compass. A few gunners tried to leap from choppers and smaller aircraft as the firewall loomed.

They didn't make it.

For more than a few out there, Bolan saw, squinting against the series of brilliant flashes, Armageddon didn't come so swift and hard.

Indeed, they were shrieking like the damned, as more fuel roared to life and began to roll them up in a tidal wave of fire. They slipped in the pooling fuel, were torched by the converging firewalls.

On the run, hell-bent on securing deeper cover as the ear-shattering blasts thundered on and men were burned alive, Bolan and Mick each hugged a hardwood before the firestorm could throw lethal shrapnel their way or the blasts knock them off their feet with seismic shock waves.

Maybe the hardmen were cursing Kuschka in their final breaths, Bolan thought, for leaving them high and dry, as the other Antonov was hammered by the wave of fire and belched apart in a thunderclap. Maybe they were wondering an instant before the fire devoured them just what the hell had gone wrong.

Not that it mattered.

Certainly the ex-KGB assassin had smelled the death trap at the last instant and was now nowhere in sight. If Kuschka and Calhoun survived, eluded him again, then that part of Bolan's plan was a dismal failure. Right then the soldier was simply concerned with riding out the destruction wrought by his own hand.

It was the picture of a total and absolute conflagration.

Mack Bolan was no doomsayer, but he couldn't help but envision a potential future where the ICBMs

were flying and raining hell on earth, a similar bang
and flash like right here, but sucking up millions in
less than a heartbeat, leaving nothing behind but their
shadows scorched into concrete from a sweeping fire
maybe as hot as the core of the sun. It was a micro-
scopic version of a nuclear fire cloud, of course, but
it did the grim job just the same in this unknown
remote corner of Borneo.

Debris began to wing through the jungle, rain on
the compound proper like giant fiery bats. Bolan
ducked as something large and heavy speared into the
tree.

The earth trembled around Bolan. A whole lot of
bad men kept shrieking and dying, and the twilit sky
over Borneo burned with the glow leaping from the
miniapocalypse.

THE SKY STOPPED falling a good two minutes later.

Mick at his rear, the Executioner moved out into
the compound proper. With a fresh 30-round clip
rammed home, the soldier fanned the carnage with
his M-16. At first search nothing stirred.

The runway was a trash heap, maybe two football
fields of fiery wreckage and bodies. Delayed explosions erupted from what was left of the motor pool.
All around him the wide dirt area of the compound
was littered with countless bodies. Smaller pieces of
wreckage thunked to earth around Bolan.

The soldier looked south, toward the jungle, and
spotted several bodies in different attitudes of death.
He then turned to the smoking maw in the main building, was about to call for Grimaldi when he saw his
friend stagger from the west end of the structure.

Blood flowed freely from a wound in the pilot's forehead. Otherwise the man seemed in one piece.

Wolf-man limped up behind Grimaldi; there was no sign of Bobby. Then Bolan watched as the merc headed toward a sprawled figure. Wolf-man bent, checked Bobby for a pulse, looked up, met Mick's stare and shook his head.

There was one hut still intact.

"Sweep the area and perimeter," Bolan called out. "I want a survivor for interrogation if possible."

Easier said than done, Bolan discovered in the next moment.

What sounded like a war cry erupted from inside the hut. Three figures charged through the doorway. Their AK-47s blazed for a moment, but they were greeted right away by four converging streams of autofire, flung back from where they came.

Bolan listened to the hungry flames, searched the killzone for several heartbeats. Then he headed for the tree line, south, where he found three corpses, facedown in the dirt. One of them had caught a shard of metal in the back of his skull. He rolled each one over with the toe of his boot. No Kuschka, no Calhoun. The soldier crouched, checked the jungle. It was dark, eerily silent deep in there, as if nature itself had been terrorized into mute paralysis by the runway apocalypse.

Bolan searched the skies. To the east, spires of black smoke cloaked the distant hills, smudged the sky that was melting into dusk. Elsewhere the sky itself seemed to ripple against the raging inferno.

It would be full night soon.

So they would go out as they had come in—leg it back to the raft, paddle downstream.

Before it hit the fan, Bolan had seen Kuschka, Calhoun and a few others bolt for this stretch of jungle. Should he pursue them through unfamiliar territory, in the dark? He was considering doing just that when he heard Mick call out. Turning, he saw a bloody figure crawling from the ruins of the main structure.

"I've got a live one, Captain—sort of."

"Grill him," Bolan called out, then left them to it as they began to question the dying man. It didn't escape Bolan's observation that Mick was far less choked up over Bobby's violent departure than Wolfman was. Chalk it up to a bigger piece of the pie, he figured, then put the merc's greed out of mind.

Bolan moved on, sweat pouring down his face as he neared the flaming scrap of the truck's cab. He went to the rear of the tracked carrier and pulled up the tarp. There were twelve missiles in all. The soldier had seen SS-20s before. They were the most formidable and feared of Russian strategic missiles. If they were nuclear tipped, they packed a punch of 150 kilotons, plenty enough to bring down a major city. Were they armed, instead, with whatever hot bioagent the enemy had been working on here? Bolan would have to raise Brognola. The big Fed would alert the proper authorities and have them secure the area.

Either way, Bolan was moving on. The final and ugly truth, he strongly suspected, was somewhere in Russia.

THE GUY HAD TAKEN several rounds to the chest and stomach. No amount of medical attention would save him; he would be dead in the next few moments.

Bolan stood next to Grimaldi, who informed him, "When it started, they went in and started to execute whoever was inside the main building. Obviously they didn't want to leave behind any loose tongues."

"Neary...Michael James..." The outstretched figure coughed up blood. "Pathologist...CDC...man in Moscow...offered me...money..."

Mick filled in some of the blanks. "Says they were brought here from Russia. Teams of Russians, some North Koreans, a couple of Americans. Bunch of Norman Glicks, Peabodys."

"What?"

"Scientists. Chem-and bio-warfare types. He says they were working on everything from a new strain of Ebola, ten times worse than what you've got in equatorial Africa. Down to chem-treated botulism, fungi and microorganisms that they grew in the laboratory here. Neary says they could eat up food supplies or get dumped in major sources of water, kill fish and people. Supposed to be loaded up in these missiles. Or they were injecting unsuspecting coworkers with what he calls hot agents, and they were to be flown to parts unknown around the world."

Wolf-man, steamed over the death of Bobby, showed no mercy as he growled at the dying man, "Any of this stuff airborne, asshole? In other words, can we catch it by breathing?"

"No...not yet...were working on it...Dayaks... used Dayaks as guinea pigs..."

"Who's your contact in Russia?" Bolan demanded.

"Pharmaceutical...medical　　supplier...company... Dukovny...took us...to Far East...remote...com-pound... underground..."

Bolan felt his blood race, knew he was on to a lead

was located. Still his mind reeled with the horror of what was revealed here. Paid coconspirators, unwitting or otherwise, injected with a fatal virus, flown to different countries, to contaminate unsuspecting populations? Viruses and bacteria born and bred to wipe out major food supplies, destroy the ecosystem?

"Where in the Far East?"

"Coast...line...think...in...land...Ok...ho... We have...no cure...were supposed...verge of antitoxin..."

Sea of Okhotsk? Bolan wondered, and posed the question, but Neary's head lolled to the side and the man looked off into space with the final stare.

Wolf-man glanced at Bobby, and said to Bolan. "Is this what you call a wrap?"

Mick was looking to the flaming runway. "Got to tell you, Captain, I wish you had saved us at least a twin engine."

"You knew the score coming in. We leg it back."

"Yeah, well, Captain, I don't get all warm and fuzzy over the thought of going back through the jungle, paddling downstream—though now I guess I can use the outboard motor, but even still—at night, four pale faces with a bunch of terrified Dayaks on the prowl. A poison dart from one of their blowguns will kill you just as easy as a bullet."

"We risk it. I don't see where we have a choice."

Someone, Bolan found out a moment later, did have a choice.

It was a faint whine at first, and all eyes turned east. A sleek jet soared over the hills, streaked on, then vanished north by northwest.

Kuschka. Calhoun. Bolan gritted his teeth. Once again the enemy had an escape route in reserve.

The Executioner met Grimaldi's angry stare. The silence between the Stony Man warriors spoke loud and clear. Next time...

As WOLF-MAN HAD so bitterly put it, it was far from being wrapped up, at least on Bolan's end.

Russia waited.

First Bolan and Grimaldi needed to get out of the Borneo jungle, get to the radio console they had moved to Pinchinko's jet and touch base with Brognola.

They double-timed it back to the tributary. Aware his enemies were either dead or had flown on, Bolan and company, with the help of NVD goggles to lead the way, moved hard and fast through the jungle.

Bolan was aware of the jungle coming to life from somewhere in the dark heart of the rain forest. In fact he spotted the darting shadows, maybe six in all, outlined in the green tunnel of his NVD goggles.

They forged on, tearing through vines, brush and foliage, Bolan feeling an itch between his shoulder blades, waiting for the first poisoned dart to strike. The only sound among the four was Wolf-man wheezing as he lugged Bobby along in a fireman's carry.

They made the raft in short order, every man aware an angry Dayak could have deflated their last means of reaching the gunboat. The raft was untouched; maybe superstition held the headhunters in check.

For the moment, at least.

They were far from home free. Bolan sensed the jungle teeming with shadows, alive with some primal anger. After all, foreigners had gone there and taken the Dayaks as nothing more than cannon fodder, something to be used, to be infected with a virus, experimented on.

Mick cranked up the outboard engine, and they headed downstream a moment later. They hit the shoreline with flashlights, roving beams outlining the dark silhouettes.

Wolf-man, either in a rage over the loss of his comrade or in a blind panic, sprayed the jungle with a long burst of Galil fire. Bolan considered knocking the weapon out of the man's hand, but let him go on, knowing he was in a situation where it could all blow up in his face, hired guns turning on him. He suspected Wolf-man did little more than further terrify the Dayaks with his shooting and cursing.

They made the gunboat in one piece.

And Bolan found his Pinchinko problem had been solved.

From the stern the soldier heard Mick whistle as his flashlight shone in the cargo hold.

"What is it?" Bolan asked, scanning the shoreline, spotting a dozen shadows or more crouched in the bush.

Mick answered by silently hauling out Pinchinko's body minus the head.

Not waiting for a response or order from Bolan, Mick casually dumped the body over the side, then moved to the wheelhouse as Wolf-man raised the anchor with the touch of a button amidships. The mercs were eager to get far away from the jungle, the darkness and the prowling Dayaks. It was understandable.

When the engines gunned to life, the jungle burst with Dayak rage.

Bolan and Grimaldi hit the deck as darts whistled overhead or thunked off the hull. Wolf-man manned the .50-caliber machine gun and cut loose with the weapon on a howl of mindless rage.

The Dayaks weren't Bolan's enemy. In fact they were the innocent, and deserved to be left alone from there on in peace.

Bolan hollered across the deck, "Stop firing! Cease firing!"

The gunboat was swinging to port, Wolf-man cursing Bolan and holding back on the trigger, sweeping lead indiscriminately all over the jungle when the Dayaks reached out to end Wolf-man's murderous fury.

Within seconds the merc's neck and face looked like a pin cushion. He jerked, still firing, holding on even as the poison set in. Finally he collapsed in a heap, his weight rattling the spent casings on the deck as he flopped around in death throes.

Moments later the darts stopped hitting the hull. Bolan looked up over the rail. Several small shadows had emerged from the jungle, now standing on the banks, blowguns low by their sides.

The gunboat gathered speed and surged on into the night.

Mick burst out of the wheelhouse, looked at the sprawled and twitching form of Wolf-man, then sought Bolan out with a level gaze.

"What the hell happened?"

No concern there. Bolan was about to tell him he'd just landed the last slice of the pie, but saved his comment.

Mother Russia was on his mind.

16

Russia

"You have failed—and miserably so, Comrade
Kuschka. By attempting to gain us some much needed
assistance in men and matériel, well, you have all
fallen way short and jeopardized our agenda. Comrades, we are at the eleventh hour, our darkest hour.
Our enemies are soon to be knocking on our back
door."

They stood at attention in a large dark hall that
struck Calhoun as medieval with its high stone walls,
the hanging battle-axes and swords, the empty armor
of warriors standing along the walls, with torchlight
wavering behind the three grim shadows at the long
oak table.

The bald, fat Russian, flanked by two dour-looking
older men, had just made several classic understate-
ments of this century, hell, the next millennium, Calhoun thought.

Calhoun could already envision his own firing
squad.

They were weaponless, for one thing, and down to
ten men who had survived the latest of the series of
brutal fiascos, sent running from the jungles of Borneo. Calhoun briefly recalled the transition from the

jungle killing ground to this large building somewhere north of Moscow, felt it clinging to his memory like a stinking shroud.

Their nemesis had once again nearly blown them off the face of the planet, had come in silent and hard, planted plastique all over the airfield, motor pool, released the fuel from the giant bins, chased them with interlocking fields of fire for the deathtrap. If it wasn't for Kuschka, whiffing the fuel at the last second, grabbing him and hauling him toward the jungle, Calhoun knew he would have been spread all over Borneo in countless dismembered pieces. As it was, he had lost a few more good men, shot or blown up while they had made their fighting withdrawal from the jungle compound.

They'd managed to escape, and after crossing maybe eight time zones, they had landed at an airfield near Moscow, nearly a full day later. Going in from the airfield in big luxury vehicles, Calhoun had been close enough to Moscow to see the spires of the Kremlin, Saint Basil's Cathedral. History and scenery were the last things on his mind. He wished he were somewhere else, anywhere but trapped in Moscow, aware that he was, indeed, at the doorstep of his darkest hour.

It all boggled his mind. How many countries had they been chased to and from? How many soldiers lost? How many deals soured, money, matériel gone, seized? Only four men, including himself, comprised the American part of the frontline troops. Calhoun had never felt more alone and scared in his life. He didn't mind admitting the fear to himself. Fear was good; it motivated. And at some point he would need all the incentive he could marshal to free himself of this madness.

Now they were being called upon to offer up some explanation for all their failures, not to mention their courage and resolve seemed in question. Calhoun noted the six AK-47-toting guards standing near the huge double doors. Was this the end? he wondered. A bullet in the head for all his trouble, his fighting nearly around the world against an unknown enemy, years of investing in arms, drugs, mercenary troops, handing out intelligence to drug lords, warlords?

Calhoun silently urged Kuschka to say something, anything.

Finally the ex-KGB assassin cleared his throat. "Many things would appear to have gone wrong. I have no excuse. I can offer no explanation. Should you see fit, should you believe that we are of no more use to the Coalition, then I offer you our lives and the lives of my American comrades."

Calhoun nearly bit his tongue in rage and terror. The bastard was giving up. Or was he? Was this some form of psychological warfare?

The silence was deafening in the hall. The bald man scanned some papers. At great length he said, "We have lost our operation in the Philippines, five of our top men, including two former generals from our Supreme High Command, killed in an attack on the hotel there. An attack, if my reports are correct—and I have no reason to dispute them—by two men, one in a helicopter gunship, the other going into the hotel, throwing grenades and spraying automatic weapons' fire around at will. Two men who, for all my own contacts and intelligences sources, remain unidentified and, it would seem, at large. Worse still, our moneyman in Manila has disappeared, his home attacked and razed, his businesses attacked and left in shambles, two important members of our business associates gunned down by a sniper. We have international law-enforcement agencies right now tearing apart our World Bank Center, which means many of our legitimate contacts and connections will fall, and they will talk.''

He looked Kuschka dead in the eye. ''The list of your troubles worldwide is most distressing. I believe your troubles have now become ours. However, I believe things are still salvageable. You will be flown immediately to our compound in the Far East. There, arrangements have been made to attempt to mobilize what forces we have, reestablish our contacts in the targeted counties, and this includes mobilizing troops and weapons of mass destruction likewise to the Ukraine. At this point we are going to roll the dice, shall we say. I see no alternative. Our proverbial backs are to the wall. As we speak, the authorities in the Kremlin are set to move on us with their secret counterrevolutionary force.''

''You are saying the compound may be attacked?''

''If it is, believe me, you are to die defending it. Am I making myself clear?''

''Yes.''

''There are those around the world we have bought and paid for and who are still ready and willing to accept us and our matériel into their countries. The North Koreans, though, wish us to step up our time-table for delivery. You will assist them personally. As for the Americans, I will ask you now, Comrade Major, if you are prepared at this late hour to sacrifice your life and if your men will likewise sacrifice their lives, if necessary, when you reach the compound? If we are attacked, will you stand and fight to your last breath to ensure we move ahead with our agenda even if under fire from our enemies?''

What was he supposed to say? Calhoun wondered. No? Effectively they were being granted a reprieve, since all available hands were needed to fight the last stand. When he no longer served the Coalition's purpose, when the final battle was done, however it fell, he was a dead man anyway. He knew too much, had seen too much for them to let him just walk away.

''I've come this far. I don't see where there's any choice.''

''Indeed, there is not a choice for you.''

It was the end, Calhoun sensed—hell, he could smell the fear and the desperation in the air. These old men, whoever they were—former Soviet military or intelligence big shots, no doubt—were prepared to unleash whatever chemical, biological and nuclear arsenal was at their disposal. Load it up, fly it on. Their doomsday war machine was set to crank up wholesale death and destruction.

What they were proposing to implement was, of course, suicide, a final, desperate act of madness, now that it was all falling apart. They could muscle, intimidate, buy and corrupt their way into the targeted countries—North Korea, Ethiopia, Sri Lanka, a couple of the equatorial African countries, maybe a South American country or two—but the Western world wouldn't stand by and watch them take down and hold hostage the targeted countries. Oh, there would be a holocaust, all right, a nuclear fireball here and there, just to show the world they were capable and serious, maybe the unleashing of the disease they had developed and tried out on the Dayaks. It struck him as utterly insane, and it could end only in all of their deaths. And all along Calhoun just wanted a nice slice of the pie, a nest egg, his own island paradise.

Feeling a creeping despair, Calhoun almost asked for that bullet, after all, but figured where there was life...

A break would show itself. Somehow he would make a run for it. When they landed at this Far East complex, he would make his own last stand. There was still a numbered account in the Bahamas, close to seven figures. Enough money to get relocated, disappear, leave it all behind. If not, he would die in the attempt and soon enough.

The old man spoke, his voice as grim as death. "Then it is settled, Comrades. Dismissed."

"THIS IS ALL highly irregular, to say the least. Not to mention it is incredibly dangerous and stupid. And you could risk my own operation, which has taken eighteen long months to mount against this Coalition, this Hydra, as you called it."

Bolan glanced at the tall man in the black leather trench coat. His Moscow contact was a man named Sergei Gaylov. Supposedly Gaylov and another man in the apartment were members of a newly formed secret police in the new Russia. They gathered intelligence on terrorists, organized crime, tracked hijacked nuclear matériel, passed on the information to the appropriate government authorities and worked, at times, with the CIA.

Right then Gaylov, Bolan was willing to bet, would be another step to tracking down his elusive enemies and ending it finally, somewhere, on Russian soil.

All told, Bolan was feeling the miles, the wear and tear of countless engagements, the jet lag, lack of food and sleep, the adrenaline roller coaster. It had been another long haul to Russia. Grimaldi had flown them out of Borneo after a grim departure with Mick. From there, they had landed at a U.S. military base in Saudi Arabia, regrouped and contacted Brognola, who had paved their way into Russia. A CIA contact Brognola had sworn could be trusted this time around had told Gaylov about two Americans who had been hunting the same men he was after, that they would be coming, needed assistance and it was in everyone's best interests, since they were fighting the same enemy. It took some pitching on Brognola's part, but the CIA contact had helped to get Bolan and Grimaldi to Kazakhstan. There, they were met by Gaylov, who arranged for the purchase of weapons and provided invaluable intelligence about Kuschka, the Russian Mafia connection and the location of the Coalition's compound in the Far East.

Now they were in a Moscow safehouse. Twenty-four hours had passed since they had left the jungle compound behind in Borneo. When Brognola had been informed of what the two warriors had come across in Borneo, the big Fed had vowed to marshal all necessary forces and secure the compound. Bolan had no doubt that he would.

Once again it was time to dig deep for grim resolve, resume the hunt.

While Gaylov fingered his thick black mustache, Bolan and Grimaldi zipped open the military duffel bags to inspect their weapons. It was quite a cache, all of it Russian: two AK-47s, several dozen banana clips, two 9 mm Makarov pistols, custom-made to take sound suppressors, two dozen grenades, a mixed assortment of frag and incendiary. There were also two RPG-7 rocket launchers, with six warheads, and the disassembled pieces of a Dragunov sniper rifle.

Bolan saw Gaylov's companion, whom he knew as only Zev, a big, lean, crew-cut figure, pull back the curtain. Darkness had fallen over Moscow. The safe-house was in the Lenin Hills, southwest of Moscow, the highest point in the city. Across the Moscow River, in the distance, Bolan had a scenic view of the Kremlin's spires, Red Square, the lit skyline of the Russian capital.

"Problems?" Bolan asked Zev, who dropped the curtain, turned and grunted something in Russian to Gaylov.

His contacts had the bulges of pistols beneath their coats. Given all the treachery the Stony Man warriors had encountered so far, the soldier was hardly about to accept anything at face value. Sure, he would take cooperation, intelligence, hardware. But if it looked as if they were being led into a trap...

They carried the necessary forged paperwork to allow them to roam at large around Moscow, but when the shooting started—and Gaylov had already provided them with a shopping list of the key members of the Dukovny family, businesses, houses, their daily agendas, from where they dined to where they met with their mistresses—anything could happen.

Bolan and Grimaldi were set to roll.

"The problem is the situation you bring to us," Gaylov said. "You are proposing to go after one of the members of the Russian Mafia, and the Dukovnys are considered just about the strongest."

While Gaylov did his concerned pitch about the

Russian Mafia, Bolan continued to inspect their weapons. He'd heard it all already from Brognola—how there were at least thirty major Russian crime groups; how after twenty years of operating and entrenching themselves primarily in the United States and Europe, they had gone global. No intelligence or law-enforcement agency could even give a ballpark figure on how many worked for, or were involved in dealings with the *mafiya*. The criminal groups worked together with the Colombian drug cartels, sold the Colombians everything from shiploads of AK-47s to submarines and helicopter gunships, largely in exchange for cocaine, which fed the growing epidemic in the new democratic Russia. The Russian Mafia was extremely difficult to infiltrate because of language barriers and cultural differences and was protected by corrupt law-enforcement officials and politicians.

"We both agree that Dukovny Incorporated," Bolan said, "is linked to NorAmAsian and that we've followed the trail here to Moscow. Simple math. Two and two."

"That, and I know Dukovny has been flying guns, even stolen fissionable nuclear matériel from the Ukraine to the Far East. He is a known associate of this Petre Kuschka. Together they made a fortune dealing with the Colombian cartels, and they have flooded Russia with narcotics. I know much about the operation of our adversaries. I also know about their recent misadventures, such as a ship of a billion dollars plus of cocaine that was bombed by a fighter jet and sunk to the bottom of the Caribbean."

Bolan felt the man's eyes all over him, but showed no reaction.

"How, may you ask, can I see the players in our immediate future, their names, whereabouts, intentions? First, even though Russian history portrays us as a cunning, diabolical people, who love our secrets, our suffering, our tragedies, nothing much has changed since the invention of democracy, a sad and sorry joke, might I add. Still the masses suffer while the rich grow richer and the corruption spreads like the arms of an octopus. There are very few secrets in Russia that remain secret for long. We live for the next upheaval. Anyway, as we speak, one of the enemy, a former colonel in Spetsnaz, was captured by my people two days ago in Moscow. His name was on this disk. And he has already confirmed much of what is on here."

Gaylov showed Bolan a floppy disk.

"We have known for some time a major revolutionary force, made up of former KGB officers, intelligence officers from the GRU and the former Soviet Supreme High Command, among others, have been plotting to overthrow the new democracy of Russia. A former colonel in Spetsnaz had left this disk behind in his apartment. We knew of Aleksandr Nikoly because he informed a comrade of his in Spetsnaz of what he was doing. Nikoly was gathering a mercenary army of ex-Spetsnaz commandos, many of whom had fallen on hard times and were desperate for money. I suspect Nikoly was covering his back by naming names, what he knew of the enemy's operation, where their base might be. This disk is complete with his contacts here in Russia, important men in the Kremlin who were in this conspiracy. Many have already been arrested.

"We found a transshipment point where Kuschka

and Dukovny were flying men and weapons to the Far East. It was an abandoned gulag in Siberia. Nikoly was found executed, a bullet behind the ear. This disk, I assume, was his way of getting vengeance from the grave, if it came to that. This is a copy. Provided what happens in the hours ahead, if you are not killed or picked up by the police, this disk will be yours to give to whoever your superiors are. It also lists many interesting American names in the CIA and in your military.

"Six hours. That is all you have before my transport flies for the Far East. By then, I will know more about the enemy's main compound, the layout, what I may find there. I have a team of commandos ready to storm this compound. If you return here in six hours, you will be part of the strike force. If not..."

Six hours, Bolan thought, to wreak havoc on the Dukovny organization, nail down the final loose end of NorAmAsian.

"Well, then, my comrade and I had better get to work," the Executioner said, and zipped up the large duffel bag.

The two Stony Man warriors were headed for the door, when Bolan heard Gaylov call out, "Good luck."

Bolan turned, read a hard sincerity in the secret policeman's eyes. The Executioner nodded and was out the door.

17

Three stops altogether, with just under five hours to wrap up this unfinished business before moving on to the main event.

Bolan didn't like the timetable Gaylov had dropped on them, but the soldier had no choice but to go with the program. It would be a stretch to hit the trio of targets, moving north by northwest, through Moscow proper then the outer suburbs, then doubling back to the safehouse in the Lenin Hills to hook up with the strike force set to fly off to the Far East. But with the intel the secret policeman had given him, Bolan hoped for a clean sweep, with maybe thirty minutes to spare—if they weren't cornered by the Russian authorities and if they survived the first round. In short, a whole lot of luck and skill would be needed to see them through the night.

The sense of urgency to be part of the strike force that would attack Hydra's main complex only served to drive Bolan with more grim determination.

Grimaldi guided the black Lexus northwest on Tverskaya Street, angling away from the concentric circles of streets and boulevards that fanned out from Red Square. It wasn't the first time he'd paid a blitzing visit to Moscow, and on this campaign he found the city hadn't changed much except for the obvious impact of increasing Western influence, namely fast-food restaurants that had popped up all over the city. Along the streets, in the squares and parks, there were countless homeless, shuffling through the cold night, maybe looking for a grill to sleep on or soup kitchens. Other shadows darted in the alleys or trolled the street corners, a smattering of women with painted faces and wrapped in fur and leather, pacing the sidewalks in front of cafés, bars. Bolan even witnessed several drug deals going down in full view as they rode the Moscow streets.

Democracy, indeed.

Change for the better, the soldier knew, didn't happen overnight. People were still desperate and hungry in the new Russia, drinking away their sorrows and despair. Crime and suicide were an epidemic, and cocaine and heroin were almost as abundant in Russia as they were in the West. Elsewhere, the former Soviet States were in disarray, collective farms abandoned in the countryside because the corrupt politicians had grabbed up the money and the land. Dismantled nuclear warheads weren't scrapped, after all, finding their way onto the black market. Terrorists of all ethnic persuasions held down their piece of hotly contested turf, sniping at the army patrols rolling through their remote villages.

Bolan turned his grim thoughts toward his objective. The soldier was under no illusions that he could crush the Russian Mafia in Moscow in a few short hours. They were too many, too organized, too deeply entrenched in Russian society. But for now Bolan would settle for the heads of the Dukovnys.

He was about to do battle with an old and very familiar enemy. Change the land, the culture, the language and the names, and it all boiled down to organized crime, hiding behind bribery, extortion, murder and intimidation. Whatever the mask of legitimacy it wore, whatever fancy suits it cloaked itself in, however large the numbered bank accounts, the villas, the luxury vehicles, it was still Animal Man at its worst. Sometimes the illusion of respectability made it even all the more horrible, made the savage even more savage when it came time for a long overdue reckoning.

Bolan was there to set the record straight, make no mistake.

He could have stayed behind with Gaylov, maybe even helped his Russian allies walk their stool pigeon through the interrogation that would pave the way for an all-out assault on the main complex of an enemy he had chased nearly around the world.

The soldier knew he would better serve his cause by tracking down and crushing the end players of NorAmAsian in Moscow, instead of sitting on his hands while the stoolie spilled his guts. Gaylov, he suspected, was perfectly capable of getting what information they needed to put the finishing touches on a strike plan against the international conspiracy that was housed in the Far East.

The word was solid on Vasily Dukovny, at least, a combination of ironclad intelligence gathered from both Brognola and Gaylov, and it made Bolan's war plan that much easier. The Russian mob boss was holding hands with Kuschka—and had been business partner with the late Benny Pinchinko—to flood Russia with narcotics, weapons and young women stolen and sold out of the Philippines. That had been one hundred percent confirmed by Gaylov. It all came complete with pictures of the mob boss and the ex-KGB assassin schmoozing and passing a fat manila envelope between them on a Moscow street corner, restaurants, bars, the pictures taken as recently as six months earlier.

The soldier might not completely dismantle the Dukovny organization, but he could make a major dent in their operations, leave them scrambling to fill a void, maybe create a rivalry with other organizations that might smell the blood and the desperation and go hunting for a bigger slice of the pie.

Down the wide boulevard, beyond a new and fashionable hotel, Bolan spotted the restaurant.

"You sure you don't want me to move in from the front?"

From the shotgun seat, Bolan turned and looked at his friend. It was just about time to start the new blitz, and Bolan became aware of the awkward positioning of the AK-47, slung across his shoulder, barrel snug against his leg beneath the long, loose-fitting trench coat. The sound-suppressed Makarov was his backup piece.

Bolan appreciated Grimaldi's concern, his willingness to be there when the hit went down, cover his back, make sure he made it out in one piece. They had come a long way in this one, together almost since the beginning, covering each other, seeking out and engaging, destroying the enemy soldiers wherever they turned up, uprooting, annihilating, chasing them down to the far corners of the earth, with more than a few near misses between them. There were always those two bullets with their names on them, Bolan knew, but they were warriors. If death was in the cards, then they would go down fighting, and damn sure take as many of what remained of the enemy as possible. No matter what, Bolan knew they would somehow finish it together. Whether they went down in a tangled heap by enemy bullets or walked on in one piece from the final killing field...

Bolan pushed aside any visions of either himself or his friend buying it.

It was time to gear it up.

"This one's solo. I want it done in about three seconds. I'll be in touch," Bolan said, and slipped the walkie-talkie into a coat pocket.

A moment later Grimaldi stopped near the mouth of an alley beside the restaurant, backed the vehicle in.

THE PLACE WAS CALLED the Bear's Head, and it was owned by Gregor Dukovny, the elder of the two sons.

Bolan had no trouble picking the lock and opening the steel door, grateful for well-oiled hinges for a change. It was a back entrance, meant for daytime deliveries, or maybe the clandestine shipping out of narcotics, prostitutes, suitcases bulging with cash when the sun went down.

On that night the only thing being delivered was certain death by a lone tall American who had the smell of the blood of his enemies in his nose, a scent growing stronger with each passing minute.

Bolan gave the Lexus, its lights out and parked in the mouth of the alley with the engine running, a final look. Grimaldi's dark shape barely outlined in the soft glow of a streetlamp, the nose of the vehicle pointed out, ready for a hasty exit.

The AK-47 up and leading the way Bolan ventured through the doorway. A quick search beyond revealed it was clear of unwanted parties. He closed the door behind him but left it slightly ajar. Down the dark narrow hall, he heard the faint sounds of voices speaking in Russian, the soft clatter of trays, music.

It was no coincidence Bolan was going after the two sons first and saving the father for last.

The old man had his origins in the KGB's Thirteenth Directorate, the old department notorious for assassinations, sabotage, all the brutality and ugliness of wet work. Specifically he had done an extensive tour of duty during the Afghanistan war. There—confirmed by Gaylov—he had committed genocide against the mujahideen alongside Kuschka with the help of chemical agents. Eventually they opened up the heroin pipeline that was the main source of his income behind the facade of being a restauranteur with first-class, four-star restaurants in Moscow and other major Russian cities. Of course, Dukovny had gone legitimate in the later years, branching out into computers, telecommunications, the cable market in Russia. Hence NorAmAsian. And more narcotics, more white slavery. Over the years the Dukovny organization had linked up with the Colombian drug cartels, most notably with the late Señor Maldonado out of Cali. Bolan could only imagine the old man's outrage when he had learned his shipment of cocaine was sitting at the bottom of the Caribbean.

All told, the pieces were starting to come together for Bolan—the Colombian connection, the rogue CIA-KGB element, the Dukovny organization, everyone in league, patting one another on the back, while advancing their own personal agendas. In short, though, what Bolan was dealing with was little more than a collection of thugs, drug dealers, international whoremongers and gunrunners with mad schemes of world domination. Dangerous thugs, to be sure.

The old man had given his elder son ownership of the Bear's Head in Moscow, as well as other duties such as money laundering, narcotics trafficking, extortion, prostitution.

Bolan rounded the corner, found no one obstructing his path as he headed for the lights of the dining room. Coming through the archway, he took in the sights. Soft music played, violins from the sound of it, beyond the beaded curtains that led to the main dining room where the guests were separated from their host. Just as he had been informed by Gaylov, the soldier found Gregor Dukovny eating dinner with his flunkies. Same hour, on the hour, same booth, every day.

The Executioner found his targets sitting alone, against the wall, in a circular booth, far corner to his right. Packed tight, the rats sat in a row, their daily routine and arrogant exclusion from the masses about to seal their doom.

Three hardmen with noticeable bulges beneath their expensive jackets came to attention at the sight of the unexpected arrival. They dug for their side arms in the next instant when Bolan pulled out the AK-47.

Gregor Dukovny, Bolan glimpsed, was a handsome, dark-haired man in his midthirties, well-groomed, a neatly manicured hand lifting a forkful of filet mignon to his mouth. Six other suits, three of whom Bolan identified from Gaylov's photos as business associates of Dukovny's, known for helping with the distribution end of heroin, were chomping down on an assortment of seafood and steak.

At first the gangsters were oblivious to the threat,

a ravenous focus fixed solely on their heaped and steaming plates. Then they definitely knew something was wrong when the bodyguards were shouting, clawing for hardware. And they nearly choked on their dinner as a group when they spotted the big invader.

Bolan cut loose with autofire.

He dropped the three hardmen as Makarov pistols were just clearing their jackets. Holding back on the Kalashnikov's trigger, Bolan raked them with a steady stream of 7.62 mm slugs, nailing them to the wall.

The bodyguards out of the way, Bolan moved on, his AK-47 resuming its deadly tracking path. His targets were now leaping to their feet, food flying, plates crashing, the suits screaming in Russian, throwing up their hands.

Bolan had no time to waste, and certainly no mercy to spare.

He emptied the clip, hosing them down with lead manglers, casting them this way and that, sending them tumbling to the carpet under their fancy dinners.

Bolan drew his Makarov, heard the screaming and stampeding of feet beyond the archway. A waiter poked his head inside. The Executioner sent him running with several wild rounds that drilled the wall above his head.

Before anyone else decided to investigate, Bolan made a fast exit, going out the way he'd come in.

He checked his watch, mentally calculating the distance to his next stop. Fifteen minutes, give or take, depending on traffic, and a whole lot of luck in steering clear of the authorities.

Either way, they were on the clock and it was ticking down.

No way in hell would the soldier miss that flight out to the Far East.

18

Round two on the short hit list would prove a tougher test, but Bolan already expected each of the next two blitzes to throw back some serious heat in their faces. The easiest kill was out of the way.

They had cleared the slaughter at the Bear's Head without incident, delay or interception. On the move again, Bolan briefly recalled the milling and frightened throngs as they eased past the crowded sidewalk in the Lexus, falling in behind the traffic.

Bolan had done the drill so many times he had factored in human nature as his main cloak to steer them free for the second leg before the home stretch. To many back at the Bear's Head, the killings might look like a gangland slaying, and that was one of Bolan's intentions—to give the impression to whoever survived the night in the Dukovny organization that a rival gang was looking to move up the pecking order.

Walking free from a slaughterbed like that, in public view, wasn't as difficult as it might appear. It happened all the time, in gangland hits in New York, Chicago or drive-bys in ghettos, where the homeboys and the crack dealers shot each other up on a regular basis—and no one saw a thing, Officer. When the shooting started in a situation like that, Bolan knew innocent bystanders, any potential witnesses were usually busy scurrying from the line of fire, fear and panic and the instinct for self-preservation taking hold, so that more often than not eyewitnesses all saw something—and someone—different if they saw anything at all.

If the shooter kept his wits, moved quickly and casually, didn't look anybody in the eye, he could vanish from the scene, leaving behind nothing but confusion and chaos, the ghost of a terrible memory.

So far—and Bolan kept his fingers crossed their vehicle hadn't been marked—their luck was holding.

Be that as it may, there was still a long way to go before they settled up with the Dukovny organization.

It was a short run up Tverskaya, melting into thickening traffic, crawling along, past theaters, the Peking Hotel, following the broad avenue until it ended at Byelorusskaya Square. One side street over Bolan found the address of the second target in short order.

They rolled down an alley adjacent to the target, parked, killed the engine, stepped out and moved in. In the distance Bolan heard the trains thundering out of the Byelorusskaya train station, the rumble of jumbo jets hurtling to points unknown from the international airport.

The squat one-story stone affair was, on paper, the accounting office for Dukovny, Inc. The hard skinny put the place as a storehouse for heroin, cash and weapons. According to Gaylov, as many as a dozen gunmen could be on hand at any given time, protecting their boss, ordering out for dinner, moving cash or merchandise.

Thus, with those numbers in mind, Bolan and Grimaldi, had stuffed two frag grenades and one incendiary canister each in the pockets of their coats.

Their intel had it the younger son, Constantin Dukovny, was a workaholic who believed he was snubbed by the old man somehow—sweating out the long hours over the family business in this building, nearly around the clock, shuffling the paperwork, moving around and padding the numbers in their books, making the calls to clients and distributors—while the elder son reaped the glory of Constantin's labor and rubbed elbows with the heads of other crime organizations, loved large, played free and ate like a king.

Only Constantin didn't know his only brother was now choking on his last supper.

Or perhaps the bad news—or good news, depending on the younger sibling's true feelings for Gregor—had traveled fast. Meaning the troops could be on high alert.

So be it.

Supposedly the Dukovnys were so brazen, so protected by corrupt law-enforcement officials and politicians they had no fear of arrest. Again, supposedly there were no lookouts, no hidden cameras, motion sensors mounted on or around the building. There would be an alarm, most likely, but anyone foolhardy enough to break into the place after hours and help himself to drugs and cash would be found floating in the Moscow River.

Making noise was the least of Bolan's concerns.

The Executioner was going in hard, leaving nothing to chance. He moved toward the back door, gave the alley a hard search, found he was alone. It was another service entrance for whatever the Dukovnys serviced.

Grimaldi had already disappeared around the edge of the alley. The Stony Man pilot would attach a thumb-sized piece of C-4 to the doorknob of the front entrance, blow it, then go in blasting.

Bolan checked his watch and knew Grimaldi was in place by then. The doomsday numbers ticked off, and the soldier lifted his AK-47, triggered a short burst that blew off the knob, shattered the lock.

Arming one of his F-1 grenades, Bolan kicked the door in and spotted three armed figures already racing down the hall. He pitched the metal egg as gunfire sprayed the doorway, crouched around the corner and rode out the ensuing blast. They screamed and their weapons fell silent.

The Executioner surged forward, the stench of blood and other leaking fluids piercing his senses. He searched for targets and didn't have to wait long. They were already scrambling out of the office, armed with assault rifles, obscured somewhat by drifting smoke and raining plaster.

During his own thundering entrance, Bolan hadn't heard Grimaldi likewise make his deadly presence known. They were in sync again, and they had the enemy running, confused and scared.

The Executioner cleared the back hall, crouched by a partition as he looked out at a sprawling office of computer banks, file cabinets, phones. Across the office, off to his left flank, he saw that Grimaldi was already in, stepping past a twitching corpse and hosing them with sweeping AK autofire. Brief return fire sought Grimaldi, but the two warriors beat them to it, flinging their shock and outrage back into their faces with sweeping bursts, turning mouths vented and shouting obscenities into death masks, as four gangsters absorbed lead, dancing crimson sieves before they pitched to the floor under withering gunfire.

With a fresh clip slapped into the AK-47, Bolan picked it up a notch, knew they were close to nailing it down. He held back on the trigger and sent another three hardmen, popping into view across the office, flying over desks, slamming into computers, sliding across the tiled floor. The Russians had been caught in a cross fire, but two gunmen were hunched in the open doorway of a cubicle about twelve yards off Bolan's flank. They were spraying the room at random with AK autofire, then tracked Bolan's position. Bullets thudded through the partition above the soldier's head, slugs tugging at his scalp.

Grimaldi bolted ahead, secured cover behind another large metal desk, firing over the corpse stretched on top of it, and nailed a guy with a machine pistol. The gunner screamed, spun and plunged through the window of another cubicle.

Bolan armed his second frag grenade, as computers sparked and blew in front of him, and gave it an underhand pitch so it rolled in the doorway near the two hardmen who could create potential standoff.

"Fire in the hole!" Bolan shouted at Grimaldi who ducked to avoid being hit by any flying shrapnel.

They saw it coming, but they were a millisecond too late in making their dash for life. The steel egg blew, taking out the wall of the cubicle, hurling more glass and steel shards across the office. The two hardmen were lost to Bolan's immediate view as the fireball kicked them out of sight, deep into the shattered cubicle.

It was then, breaking cover, straining through the ringing in his ears for sounds of life, Bolan spotted the younger Dukovny.

And Constantin Dukovny was a bloody mess. The young gangster had been handsome, like his late brother, as Bolan recalled the intel pictures, but half his face was now crimson hamburger where steel bits of shrapnel had chewed off pieces of flesh.

Bolan rolled out into the smoke and the sparks while Grimaldi covered him.

Only the wheezing of Constantin Dukovny broke through the ringing in Bolan's ears. The gangster crawled on his belly for a discarded AK-47. He reached out a bloody hand, turned his partially mutilated face and snarled in Russian, "Who are you?"

"The end of the line," Bolan told him.

Dukovny balked, switched to English and repeated the question.

"I understood the first time," Bolan growled.

"Why? What do you want?"

"Just a little gentler and kinder world, and you don't fit the picture," the Executioner stated, triggering a short burst into Dukovny's skull as the man's fingers closed around the AK-47.

Bolan then gave Grimaldi the nod. Both men pitched their incendiary canisters into opposite far corners of the office, then beat a hasty retreat out the back door.

They reached the alley as the canisters thundered from inside.

Two down, one to go.

The night was shaping up, but there was one last stop to make.

If nothing else, old man Dukovny would live another hour, ninety minutes at the outside, with the bitter knowledge there was no living blood to inherit the kingdom.

THE OLD MAN SAW the dining room spin, go dim, as if his brain were winking out with what he'd just heard, the mind unable to grasp much less comprehend the horror. Nausea then boiled in his belly, and he thought he would pass out. Instead, the phone, feeling like some great weight all of a sudden, slipped from his fingers.

He felt the tears of rage and grief burning up from the core of a brain that felt as if it were on fire.

He stood on legs of rubber, teetered, then moved for the bar. His lips trembled, and the bile squirted up his throat.

He became numb with disbelief, horror, choked down the vomit.

The word had reached him from one of his lieutenants in Moscow.

His sons were dead. His only living blood had been gunned down—by whom? And why? As if the questions were even important.

He poured himself a glass of vodka, choked it down, liquor hitting the bile in his throat. He was alone in the dining room, but he felt like the last man on earth, even with his twenty-man security force scattered around the mansion. He was an old man, at the end of the line...with no family. With nothing.

He wanted to weep, but his thoughts hardened with a sudden craving for revenge. What was done was done. It was time to act, to strike back. Still, how could this have happened? his mind screamed, the fury and the anguish building again, a time bomb in his churning belly. Reports were that a lone gunman had walked into the restaurant he had given as a gift to his elder son, gunned down Gregor, his bodyguards and their business associates, just strolled off, vanished into the night without a trace. Then Constantin and his crew, not even thirty minutes later. Gunned down, blown up where they sat in their office, not a single eyewitness to the massacre.

He racked his brain for a clue as to who would declare war on him. He did business with several organizations, but everything was running smooth lately, everyone getting richer, and with his legitimate tie-in with NorAmAsian…

"Damn!"

Vasily Dukovny caught a glimpse of his sagging features and bald dome in the mirror, bellowed and hurled the glass at the image. The mirror shattered. The doors opened, but he didn't acknowledge his men bursting in with AK-47s and sweeping the dining hall as if they were under attack.

Pinchinko, he thought. The trouble in Manila. His own men had been reported killed in the Philippines, hit by a sniper when they'd gone to pick up their cash tribute. And Kuschka? Somehow it was all connected; there was a power play at work. Well, Dukovny knew all about the KGB killer's past, and his recent troubles. He had been in Afghanistan, after all, many lifetimes ago, right alongside the man where they had plotted and carried out the wholesale slaughter of mujahideen villages, spraying the peasant masses with nerve gas from the air. His beginnings in the Afghanistan war with Kuschka had quickly led to the opening up of a safe passage to Moscow for the distribution of heroin.…

It all had something to do with narcotics, he was sure.

And his lone source of cocaine, Maldonado, was dead. Maybe the Colombians had landed in Moscow and were looking for answers, or vengeance against himself or Kuschka or both. The shipment of narcotics that he had invested in with Kuschka had supposedly been blown up by a fighter jet. Or had Kuschka been lying about that, stringing him along, looking to cut him out, keep the drugs? And his own private jets, worse still, aiding Kuschka, who bought and paid for the fissionable nuclear matériel he stole out of the Ukraine, the SS-20s he had acquired through his own former KGB contacts, helping the KGB killer with whatever scheme he had in mind. And now this treachery. Another slap in the face, no doubt.

His sons were dead.

Oh, there were plenty of possibilities as to the identities of the murderer of his sons. Too many.

It was time to act.

In fact Dukovny determined he would take to the streets of Moscow himself and hunt down the man or men responsible. And if it turned out Kuschka was responsible for the horror of this night, Dukovny would fly all the way to the Far East and kill the man himself.

He swept past his bodyguards, was opening a panel in the wall and hauling out an AK-47 when he heard the shouting, followed by an explosion rocking the compound.

The old man stood rooted, listening to the sounds of cursing and shouting, the panic coming from the south. Then it sounded as if the mansion would come down as still more explosions thundered around the complex.

The old man clenched his jaw, slapped a clip into the assault rifle and cocked the bolt. His sons were dead, and it appeared as if the killers had come to claim the father. Good enough.

Vasily Dukovny had nothing to lose.

NOTHING TRICKY, nothing fancy about the home-stretch blitz, since the Stony Man warriors were going for a clean sweep, total annihilation of the old man, his hardforce and, if necessary, the destruction of the mansion.

Moments earlier, Bolan and Grimaldi had secured a vantage point on the edge of a low hill, south of the mansion, surveyed the compound, taken in the numbers and made the attack strategy on the spot.

It had eaten up the better part of an hour to get to this dark countryside of cottages, churches and scattered villages north of Moscow. The Executioner found that the layout of the Dukovny estate was similar to the many mansions, villas and other compounds they had attacked and razed: sprawling grounds, wrought-iron fence, polished marble and stone, floodlights; isolated, with a stretch of woods, low hills, the nearest eyes and ears, according to the map, a village about two miles east.

The motor pool near the pillared front entrance was the second thing to go, along with seven or so hardmen lingering around the vehicles.

Bolan put down the Dragunov sniper rifle with fixed sound suppressor and picked up his AK-47. He'd retrieve the sniper rifle on the way back, if they made it that far. Evidence of four long-range kills were sprawled on the ground, one at the front gate, three who had been patrolling to the west.

No sooner had number four gone down than someone at the motor pool shouted in Russian, and Grimaldi began to lob RPG warheads into the motor pool. The two blasts scythed what Bolan hoped was three-quarters of the security force, if Gaylov's intel was on the money, and at that point the soldier had no reason to dispute the information. Further, no one lived at the compound, other than the boss and his security force, who also pulled double duty as housekeepers. The old man was divorced, and not even a girlfriend was at the compound. Noncombatants weren't a factor.

They moved out, Bolan's AK-47 poised to fire, the RPG-7 slung across his shoulder. The soldier used a frag grenade to blow down the front gate, and the two warriors were through.

It was a straight-ahead charge, Bolan and Grimaldi surging up the driveway, sprinting from tree to tree. Whatever survivors showed on the driveway ahead were shadowy stick figures, staggering from the crackling flames.

Bullets sought Bolan, bark gouged from tree trunks above his head. He ducked, triggered the Kalashnikov, the short burst catching two hardmen and flinging them to the ground, near the licking tongues of fire. Three more raced from the motor pool, but the fuel tank of a luxury vehicle caught fire and the blast ripped through the trio before Bolan could take them out.

Bolan took cover behind a tree, dropped to one knee as Grimaldi moved on, skirting the edge of the firelight, his AK-47 chattering and scoring another kill on a staggering shadow near the flaming wreckage.

The Executioner lined up the RPG's sights on the massive double doors. They were opening the front entrance when he triggered the warhead, sent the missile on a true line and blew doors and man back into the building.

How many left? Was the old man even alive? Maybe running like hell from the mansion, out the back way?

Only one way to find out.

IT WAS TIME to go for broke.

Choking and gagging sounds greeted the two warriors as they crouched into the smoking maw that was the front entrance. Two corpses were stretched out in the foyer, but Bolan didn't recognize either of the dead as the old man.

AK-47 leading the way, Bolan gave Grimaldi the nod, and the soldier went in low, the ace pilot high. Beyond the drifting cloud of cordite, two figures scuttled into Bolan's view, their backs to him, their AK-47s low by their sides. Obviously they had survived a near miss with the RPG blast, were turning tail and running. Bolan and Grimaldi peeled off at the end of the front hall, cut loose on the runners at the same instant. Double lines of 7.62 mm slugs zipped up their spines and punched through the backs of their skulls. Momentum lifted them off their feet, sent them on a long slide face first over polished marble.

Bolan and Grimaldi fanned the living room with their weapons. The Executioner sensed a presence, heard short sharp breaths from somewhere, and scanned the large living room, which was cluttered with divans, antiques—

A howl of mindless rage erupted. A figure jumped up, screaming in Russian, an AK-47 flaming in his hands. Bolan and Grimaldi opened up with autofire.

It took a dozen rounds before Vasily Dukovny's aim was thrown off. Dukovny kept shouting and cursing, and Bolan heard something about "sons." The old man knew.

He took the knowledge that his kingdom had crumbled, with no inheritors, to the grave. Finally he toppled, spurting crimson from his shredded chest.

The echo of autofire in his ears, Bolan moved out, while Grimaldi covered the rear.

"Kuschka..."

Bolan heard the old man gasping the name beyond the divan. The Executioner, cautious, moved up beside the man.

A pair of glazed eyes sought out Bolan. "Kuschka...send you...kill...sons...who..."

For whatever good it would do him, Bolan told the dying boss, "It wasn't Kuschka, Dukovny. In fact Kuschka will be joining you soon."

The Executioner triggered a mercy burst into Dukovny's chest. He surveyed the living room and the front entrance for any sign of armed resistance but found none. The soldier backed out, AK-47 ready to take on any survivors just the same.

It appeared a clean sweep.

Now all they had to do was clear the hellgrounds and make it back for the main event.

19

"My American comrades, so far here is what we are looking at," Gaylov announced. "Pay attention."

Bolan sat beneath the overhead light, beside Grimaldi. The two warriors watched as their Russian contact spread out the satellite photos, the topographic maps and what looked to Bolan like the blueprints of the compound.

They were aft in the Antonov transport, the rumble of the giant turboprop engines in Bolan's ears as the air freighter—one of two—flew east for the main event.

The Executioner glanced past Gaylov at maybe fifty blacksuited soldiers, stem to stern, port and starboard, as silent and grim as death. They were smoking, napping, drinking coffee, checking weapons. Who and what exactly the commandos were Bolan didn't know, and he suspected Gaylov would only fill him in on a need-to-know basis. In order to identify friend from foe when the pitched battle began, each man would wear a black armband with a white star, the old red star of the Soviet military probably too difficult to mark in the chaos of battle at night, he figured. Bolan and Grimaldi had already been given their markers.

They had left Moscow in a hurry. Gaylov had been

silent during the ninety-minute drive to a clandestine airfield east of the city, where soldiers, canvas-covered pallets of gear and hardware were being loaded into the two Antonovs. Three MiGs were on hand, their escort out of there at that early-morning hour.

They had been airborne now for a little more than an hour. Bolan peered at the hard set to Gaylov's features, waiting for the Russian to brief them. So far, the man had said nothing about the Americans' bloody takedown of the Dukovny family. There'd been no dressing-down, no thump on the back, but Bolan had expected neither.

Never mind. The Executioner was geared up for the final stretch. That it had come to something like this didn't surprise him, nor did it hardly seem anti-climactic. Apparently, while Bolan and Grimaldi had been tearing down the enemy's operations around the world, the Russians had suspected and been preparing for some time to deal with the problem in their own backyard. If timing was everything, then Bolan and Grimaldi were right on the money. And no, he wasn't about to question this twist of fate, this last-minute stroke of good fortune. It was enough that the two warriors were there, going in, even if they were attached to a large clandestine strike force. With the enemy numbers they had faced so far, Bolan figured the two of them could use all the help they could get.

"This was an old military installation," Gaylov said, pointing at the pictures, reviewing each one with Bolan and Grimaldi. "Airfield, barracks, sat dish, APCs, jeeps, trucks, fuel bins, radar and flight tower, four MiGs that we can determine and an unknown number of assorted transport, possibly attack helicopters and two Antonovs under these tarps. Our sat photos are not X rays, so there is no telling how many aircraft are hidden under these tarps, nor could my prisoner give me an accurate number. Judging the area of the tarps, well, it would appear a considerable number of aircraft are grounded in this northern edge of the compound. Obviously they must go first.

"This compound was supposedly abandoned when the so-called cold war ended, but we've learned it has been in use by former KGB officers and members of the former Soviet Supreme High Command for some time, maybe as long as a year. It is also complete with a labyrinth of underground bunkers, mess hall, more barracks, storage areas, large work areas, where, my prisoner and my other contacts have informed me, there is a contingent of Russians and North Koreans working around the clock on nuclear, biological and chemical weapons. It has been converted, obviously, into a weapons factory. What exactly we will find there is anybody's guess."

Bolan nodded at the biohazard suits hanging near the soldiers. "I take it you're prepared in the event of the release, accidental or otherwise, of chemical or bio agents."

"Only as far as gas masks, antitoxins for the less deadly agents, such as anthrax, botulism. As for contact with any humans or blood contaminated with Ebola or some genetically mutated strain of the virus…I shudder to think. There is no cure, no antiviral shot."

"The numbers," Bolan pressed.

"A rough estimate from my prisoner put the enemy numbers at one hundred, perhaps as high as 120 men. Mostly Russians, some North Koreans. Half of the force up top, half below, if I am to believe my prisoner, and since he has been promised something comparable to your Witness Protection Program, I tend to believe him. If the enemy numbers are in that range, then the odds of success are good. I have a force of eighty men—plus you two.''

"It will be pretty awkward running around, engaging the enemy in biohazard suits,'' Grimaldi noted.

"The suits are for a team of specialists I have on the other Antonov. They are specialists in germ and chemical warfare, experienced and trained to deal with the handling of chemical and biological agents. They will go in, but only after we have taken down and secured the compound.''

"I hope you're not looking to take prisoners,'' Bolan said.

Gaylov turned grim. "No. Just as I have learned you took none against the Dukovny organization. The Russian Mafia is responsible for many of the ills that have befallen Russia. Perhaps you did little more than cut out one small piece of a festering sore, where the maggots of other crime organizations will come to feed on. I do not know. Only time will tell.''

"It was a loose end,'' Bolan told the Russian.

"I understand—the NorAmAsian connection. What you did also signaled me that you are fighters. I can count on you.''

If nothing else, the faint praise bolstered Bolan's confidence that Gaylov had fully accepted them on board the strike force. Earlier the soldier had filled their Russian contact in on the Borneo end of their mission, what had gone down in the Philippines to eventually lead the two of them into Russia. The backbone of the Dukovny organization had been broken, and NorAmAsian was more or less history.

Bolan waited for Gaylov to continue. The Russian fired up a cigarette. At the end of their flight, they would land at a compound, sometime late the next afternoon, take the final briefing, then be flown by helicopter farther east to the foothills of the Kolyma Mountains. It was wild frontier country, remote, cold, barren, Gaylov said, the closest link to civilization a Siberian fur-trading outpost, maybe twenty kilometers north of the complex. Skintight thermal lining would be handed out, to be worn beneath their combat blacksuits, as well as skintight gloves.

Gaylov further laid it out. There were freight elevators in buildings that the Russian indicated on his intel photos at three separate spots: one to the north at the base of the hills, another in a building midway down the compound, with another shaft at the far southern end, and stairs apparently also near all the elevators. There was a forty-foot descent to the belowground complex. Bolan said it would be wiser to use the stairs for their descent, and Gaylov agreed. No sense in letting the enemy lie in wait, catch them all packed in an elevator before the hit could get rolling.

Gaylov not only had four transport choppers on hand, but there were also six attack Mil Mi-24 helicopters that would help soften the target along with the MiGs, strafing the airfields, providing the air support while the ground force moved in, did all the damage they could at ground level before descending.

When Bolan was informed the enemy had an antiaircraft battery on the western edge of the main base, the soldier volunteered to take them out. He would circle wide to the north and come up the hill on their blind side. He had done enough silent kills to assure Gaylov he could pull it off. Gaylov thought about it and agreed. The attack would begin at nightfall, everyone checking their watches beforehand, getting into position to throw it at the enemy all at once. Radio communications, which could be intercepted, were banned once they started to hike into firing position.

"Take out the antiaircraft crew—quietly," Gaylov ordered. But then Bolan was to wait for his order to move in on the compound, let his air force inflict as much damage, as many casualties as possible. With luck the troops at ground level would be eating dinner in their barracks.

The plan was dicey, Bolan knew, but the obvious risks involved were nothing compared with the potential results. Even still, the Executioner pointed out that the enemy could decide to go out in a suicidal blaze, unleash a nuke or a chemical or biological agent when they penetrated below. Gaylov acknowledged that, but they would just have to take their chances. It was as simple as he could make the plan. A straight-on blitz. The soldier got the answer he expected, grateful, if nothing else, they were on the same page.

Bolan also believed that more often than not, the simple and direct assault was the most efficient. Of course, they would need all the tenacity they could muster, seize the initial advantage and decimate as much of the enemy as they could in the opening rounds—and find more than a little luck along the way.

Before it was over, though, there would be plenty of dead men, foe and friendly.

One look into Gaylov's eyes and Bolan knew the Russian expected casualties on their side. If the two Americans were destined this time around to go down by enemy fire, then the Executioner would see his prime targets go first.

"I want my man on one of those Hinds, with a direct radio tie-in to him also."

Gaylov looked at Bolan, then at Grimaldi. "Do you realize we were never formally introduced? Your contact told you my name, but I do not even know the names of the Americans I will be fighting beside and perhaps dying beside in less than twenty hours."

"You never asked, but I'm Belasko and this is Griswald. Well, about Griswald?"

"Fair enough, he will fly in one of the Hinds, with your own radio tie-in. I suspect he's qualified, or you wouldn't be asking."

If you only knew how much, Bolan thought.

"I will attach to you, Belasko, a seven-man squad. They all speak English, and you will be put in charge of them."

Leading a squad of commandos into battle was definitely going by the seat of the pants, but Bolan would lay it out for them again, simple and direct. They would follow orders, and he had no doubt they were capable fighters. Even still, it was baggage, being responsible for the lives of Gaylov's troops. At this point, though, there was no sense in shaking up the program.

"Your primary objective, after taking out the antiaircraft crew—which should be no more than three, four targets tops—will be to mop up any survivors at ground level, then descend from the north stairs while myself and the others go down from the other points of descent. We will seal them off, hopefully run them into each others's guns."

Bolan turned even more grim. "And Kuschka and a traitor named Calhoun we've been chasing nearly around the world?"

"If they are there, all I can tell is first come, first served. Fair enough?"

The Executioner wasn't along for a vengeance ride, but it set his teeth on edge to think he might not be the one to take down Kuschka and Calhoun. And those two had a lot of innocent blood on their hands. Whatever lay ahead in the coming hours, Bolan was hell-bent on making those two pay. He wouldn't be cheated.

"Fair enough," the Executioner agreed.

"Very good. Any questions, ask me later, when I have further ironed out any more details I have neglected. We still have a long flight ahead of us. I suggest the two of you get some sleep."

It wasn't a bad idea, Bolan thought, but he doubted that it would be little more than a restless dozing off. The men he had tracked all over the planet were at the other end of the ride; he could feel it in every fiber of his being.

EIGHTY ARMED MEN, not including the air force, waited on one man to knock out the antiaircaft battery.

Bolan was up to the task, indeed savored the responsibility.

It seemed like another eternity since they had landed, been given the final brief, choppered deeper east, drove to the appointed positions, legged it in.

The day had passed in grim anticipation.

Now it was nightfall, and the lone American was swiftly and silently moving up the gully. Bolan was heavily laden with the tools of his trade: an AK-47 had been slung across one shoulder; the RPG-7 hung down his back; his combat webbing bristled with grenades, a spare warhead for the rocket launcher, clips for his assault rifle and side arm, gas mask, walkie-talkie.

Call it instinct, experience, he knew that his enemies were somewhere on the compound grounds, above or below; it wouldn't matter in a few minutes. Nothing and no one would stop Bolan from razing the compound, if that's what it took to nail Kuschka and Calhoun.

The silenced Makarov leading the way, Bolan kept grim sights fixed on the two shadows standing guard on the ridgeline. Just beyond the quad-barreled and self-propelled ZSU-23-4 automatic cannon, Bolan saw a third shadow step from the lit doorway of a shack that he figured was the temporary outpost.

Someone up there had been chain-smoking, the orange cigarette tip glowing in the night the whole time Bolan had made the hundred-plus-yard approach down the base then up the hill. The smoker received a dressing-down from the shadow that had just moved onto the ridgeline. The cigarette flew away, and the man picked up infrared binoculars and began to survey the sky and the endless steppe, broken only by low hills to the east.

Something didn't feel right to Bolan. They were tense up there, seemed highly agitated. If there were hidden cameras in the hills, motion sensors, long-range radar that was now picking up the incoming flight of the armada, due to sweep over the compound...

Bolan checked his watch. Four minutes and counting. And he still had another fifty yards or so to get within sufficient striking distance to assure a clean sweep of the trio. Then two of the seven-man team he had left behind in a narrow pocket in the hills would man the 23 mm autocannon, rain havoc where they could on the compound while he led the other five men into battle.

The Executioner kept climbing, the stars and the moonlight providing just enough glow to keep him moving up and on without the aid of NVD goggles.

Field glasses froze suddenly. From somewhere far to the east, and growing with each passing second, Bolan heard the faint shriek of afterburning turbos.

He bit down the curse. The MiGs. They were either ahead of schedule or Bolan was behind, or the sentry up there had superhearing, or radar...

Skip it. Bolan rose up and caressed the Makarov's trigger. The sentry was lowering the field glasses, pointing west, his mouth opening when a silenced 9 mm round drilled through his temple.

Bolan had just enough edge of surprise, as his first victim crumpled, to catch them frozen for a heartbeat, squeeze off two 9 mm rounds. The second, then third shadow dropped out of sight to the sound of bone cracking and yielding to the 9 mm projectile.

The Executioner was up and running. He hit the rise, crouched, fanning the ridgeline. Looking through his own infrared binoculars, the soldier gave the sprawling compound, nestled in a large valley, a quick but hard search, north to south. In the flesh the compound was far more massive and impressive than any satellite photos could detail. Along the runway there was a sudden flurry of activity, two MiGs rolling south, ready to lift off.

The enemy was already on high alert.

So much for surprise.

Then Bolan saw a force of gunmen, maybe two platoons, racing for the southern edge of the compound.

They'd been made.

Bolan got on the radio and raised Gaylov, who was in position to the south. "Rogue Force to Bear Claw One, come in."

"What is going on—?"

Bolan heard the chatter of autofire over the radio. South, he saw the shadows charging the edge of the hills at the end of the valley.

The soldier went into the shack, AK-47 poised to fire, but found the radio console unattended inside. Three had come there to guard the western perimeter, and they were out of the game.

Bolan changed the frequency on his handheld radio and called his team. They were known to him as One, Two, Three and so on. The Executioner ordered One up the rise, with Two and Three to secure the cannon. It was show time.

Then the cavalry arrived. They flew in low and hard, and Bolan felt the slipstream of the MiG fighter jets as they blew past him, spooling dust around him in their wake.

A second later the MiGs began to unload destruction on the airfield.

Bolan skirted down the edge of the rise, saw the shadows of his team ascending rapidly.

It was time to break, headlong and hard, into the thick of it.

20

The smell of fear and desperation in the underground complex nearly overpowered Calhoun. Or was it just his own sense of impending doom? His own despair, paranoia?

Forget it, he told himself. He was on his own, and it was time to take care of himself. Calhoun didn't have a clue as to what was really going on, but none of it looked or felt good. For one thing, he had been confined to quarters since landing in Kuschka's jet, then thrown with his men into a sterile white room with a stainless-steel open toilet, no food, no water.

He, along with his three surviving men, were now with Kuschka, striding behind the tall Russian, their boots drumming on the metal gangplank that overlooked a warehouse area. Below men were scurrying everywhere, frantic, it seemed, Russian rats in the maze of intersecting halls and rooms, shouting, toting AK-47s, inspecting the missiles beneath the tarps. Elsewhere, beyond the high glass-walled partition to the east, he saw the decon chambers, men in biohazard suits, shuffling through the steel doors. Armed men in black combat fatigues were grabbing and shoving guys in all directions. It looked as if they were being herded into some type of carts that were set to move on rail tracks. If Calhoun didn't miss his guess, they were either coming under siege or about to be attacked. The latter was far more feasible.

"So, where are you shipping us off to next?" Calhoun asked, unable to keep a bitter edge out of his voice.

Kuschka ignored him, and Calhoun resisted the urge to lock a forearm around the Russian's neck, squeeze until his eyes popped out, take his chances from there. Given all the activity, the armed men sweeping past him, it wouldn't take much to grab an AK-47, some spare clips and cut loose.

Either way, he was a dead man. Kuschka wanted his ass, and Calhoun had been around long enough to know the scarred Russian had turned it personal, somehow blamed him for all the fiascos, setbacks and disasters.

Oh, well, no one lived forever. And if the Coalition thought it would live to see some thousand-year reign, its backers were dreaming a dead man's dream.

Rounding a corner, they came to a large room where several old men were rolling around the radio consoles, watching the bank of cameras, stabbing at the monitor screens. They were barking at one another in Russian, then a stocky white-haired guy with a face like a potato snarled something to Kuschka. Calhoun nearly went berserk. He shouted, "In English! What the fuck is going on?"

Something was definitely wrong; the sky was about to fall again. A moment later Calhoun was sure the end had come. They were maybe fifty feet below-ground, but the thunder of the first of many explosions was clearly heard, rocked the gangplank beneath Calhoun's feet and sent him teetering into the rail like some drunken kid.

From an adjacent gangplank, Calhoun saw three black-clad figures hurling AK-47s his way.

"Look alive," Kuschka rasped as Calhoun and his trio of men caught the assault rifles. Spare clips were tossed at them a moment later. "Stay with me at all times, Major."

Calhoun almost laughed. It was over, for all of them, and the Russian was barking out orders. The hell with him. They were finished. Someone had found them out, discovered their main base and had come to shoot and blow them clear out to sea. Why wasn't he surprised? Fate had been looking to kick it down their teeth since Manhattan.

From the constant rumble of explosions above, Calhoun knew a sizable assault force had stormed the runway, the complex above, and was soon to make an entrance—guns blazing, grenades flying—belowground.

Well, Calhoun determined he wasn't finished yet, not by a long shot. They were still four of the toughest, meanest, most vicious killers Russia had seen since the Mongol hordes. If Calhoun had to, he would put a few rounds through the back of Kuschka's head, grab some wheels, hell, he'd walk out if he had to.

Then a vision of their nemesis danced through his mind and froze him for a moment before Kuschka snarled for him to follow.

And just where were they supposed to go? he wondered.

To the grave, to hell, he figured, but picked up the pace and fell in behind Kuschka just the same.

At least he was armed.

NOTHING SOPHISTICATED about it, but it was designed that way. It was a full-frontal assault, with the ground forces charging in, going for broke while the MiGs did as much damage as possible in the opening onslaught.

And the MiGs did plenty; they might have shaved the odds considerably and saved the night, as far as the opening moments of battle went.

AK-47 poised to fire, Mack Bolan led his squad onto level ground. The big American was flanked by two-man fireteams, each team ordered to fire away from him, so that they weren't shooting over or through each other. There was a sixth commando covering their rear, and he was holding back, his RPG-7 armed and ready, a satchel stuffed with the cone-shaped warheads.

The enemy MiGs almost made it off the ground when they were blown into fiery scrap by the friendly fighter jets, and not a second too soon. An air war, with the gunships on the tails of the MiGs, might have proved disastrous. Seizing and then controlling the aboveground complex was critical.

The barracks went next, a structure nearly the size of a football field, Bolan figured, and capable of housing several hundred soldiers. The mountain-sized fireball was the end result of six or seven missiles slamming into the structure before the MiGs peeled off from their initial attack. In the chaos and confusion of combat, it was hard to tell how many missiles had uprooted the building, turned it into a wavering ocean of flaming kindling.

Not that it mattered. Chaos had erupted, and bullets were flying everywhere, plenty of survivors breaking from at least two other large buildings, firing from cover behind a motor pool that consisted of several dozen vehicles.

With debris beginning to rain around them, winging off the hard-packed earth, torn bodies cartwheeling in all directions, Bolan and his team started to pick out targets.

It became a shooting gallery of prime flesh. On the run, Bolan and his commandos cut loose with their AK-47s, scythed down a wave of enemy guns who attempted to join the fray. Maybe a dozen or so enemy hardmen had surged forward, triggering weapons at them from the outer limits of the line of fireballs that thundered up and down the massive ring of aircraft, grounded beneath the tarp. It quickly became apparent to Bolan no one was flying from this one.

Before Bolan knew it, he had expended three clips and the way ahead was littered with twitching corpses. How Gaylov was faring he couldn't be sure, but out of the corner of his eye, as bullets whizzed over his head, tugged at his blacksuit, he saw two of the MiGs soaring southward, cutting loose on the enemy ground force in that direction with machine-gun and rocket fire. The third MiG had banked south, veered west, then swung around and was jetting back, with guns blazing and rockets streaking for the surviving structures, men and machines that somehow remained unscathed beyond the runway.

It was total madness, and all bets were off as to who would win, Bolan knew. Adrenaline coupled with the knowledge that the prime targets, if still alive, were somewhere in the area drove Bolan on. If that passed for hope, then it kept the soldier running.

From his left flank, Bolan spotted maybe thirty white stars bounding off the bottom of the foothills, leapfrogging boulders, racing ahead from the cover of trees, firing at anything that darted or fired from the wall of blazing fire eating up the aircraft.

It all thundered and screamed on, fire, man and metal, all the elements of earth sucked up, torn apart, hurled back.

Fuel bins and fuel trucks near the grounded aircraft erupted in fireballs from direct hits from the lone MiG, and gas tanks blew to the west and the south as the MiG scored on the motor pool with laser-precision strikes, sweeping on.

The earth shuddered as if it might open under his feet, and Bolan looked up by instinct—and saw a huge jagged sheet of something plunging for him.

The falling debris might have saved Bolan's life.

Suddenly autofire was tracking the Executioner. Stick figures, outlined in the crackling lake of fire ahead, were pouring it on with AK-47s. Bolan was forced to nose-dive to his left as the wreckage banged to earth. He was covered by the smoking debris as bullets whined off metal, gouged out divots of earth where he'd been standing just a second earlier.

From the west Bolan heard his two-man crew working the ZSU-23-4 on overdrive. They peppered anything that moved on them, or machines that started to roll from the raging tongues of fire lapping up the aircraft pool. He gave them a mental slap on the back as they rained a line of HE blasts down on the crew of hardmen, and beyond, dead ahead, maybe ten shadows who were lining them up with rocket launchers and assault rifles. The explosions tore through the second wave and their warheads flew wide of Bolan, impacted in the hills far to his rear.

The soldier got on the handheld radio to raise Grimaldi. "Rogue Force to Lone Eagle, come in."

"I'm on it, Rogue Force. We're coming up on your rear now. Suggest you hug some turf."

"Undetermined number of targets at twelve o'clock."

"Roger, already see them. I'm all over it."

Despite Grimaldi's warning to go to ground, Bolan held back on the trigger of his Kalashnikov, hosing down three dark shadows charging from the firewall, eating up the piles of rubble and sea of wreckage to the east.

Then Bolan went low, feeling the rotor wash as the two Hinds swept overhead, unloading machine-gun fire and 57 mm hell-bombs, an assortment of bigger missiles streaking away, the NATO Swatters.

Hell on earth roared on.

Three seconds later it all went to hell as men and machines took to the air on blinding saffron flashes.

The Executioner charged on, linking up with thirty commandos along the base of the northern hills, and set his sights on the freight elevator's doors, which stood open and inviting.

FEROCIOUS RESISTANCE, the kind of suicidal grandstanding Bolan had seen from terrorists too many times in the past when they knew it was over but wanted to take out as many of their perceived enemies as possible, greeted them in the massive opening at the foot of the hills.

Two dozen or so hardmen crouched in the mouth of the opening around the elevator. They were firing their AK-47s in sustained bursts and unloading RPG-7s when Bolan joined a group of his Russian comrades in hurling frag bombs to take the fight forward. If they destroyed the elevator in the process or brought the mouth of what looked like a man-made cave down on the enemy and thus impeded their progress below, then so be it.

There was no cover for the bad guys, nowhere for them to run or duck at the moment.

So Bolan, crouched behind the smoking tail of a wrecked cargo plane, let the enemy out on the runway have it with long sweeping bursts of AK-47 autofire. The Executioner scored three, maybe four kills before he dived to earth, covered his head and rode out the skull-splitting roar of thunder from the grenade blasts. He might have been all of thirty yards away, but Bolan clearly heard the screams of men being shredded by countless steel fragments, the familiar stench of cordite and blood in his nose.

His Russian allies charged forward, even as tight groups of their comrades were kicked every way by RPG blasts.

With thunder in his ears, Bolan glanced over his shoulder and saw two of the Hinds vaporized inside roiling clouds of fire. South, he saw crouched figures near the glowing tongues of fire, hefting rocket launchers. When another Hind, streaking away from the inferno, was turned to a fireball that became suspended in midair, Bolan bet they were firing heat-seeking missiles.

With a sense of urgency he called it in and was relieved a second later to hear Grimaldi's voice. As he looked up and Grimaldi laid out his incoming position, Bolan saw his friend's Hind burst through the rocketing tips of fire from the now plunging gunship wreckage. The ace pilot swooped down on the rocket teams in a long strafing run, miniguns flaming from the nose, rockets blazing off from the wings, the ensuing blasts consuming the heat seekers.

With the roar of autofire and the angry crackle of fire in his ears, the soldier headed for the elevator when something strange caught his eye.

Fifty yards away, right beside a rippling line of fire along the runway, the ground opened up. Bolan watched as what appeared to be two trapdoors swung up, over and flattened on the ground. Then a boxlike structure rose from the earth as if by magic.

An elevator, one not on the blueprints.

He wasn't sure how he knew or why, but he wasn't surprised when several seconds later, the doors parted and out stepped four shadows, two of which he recognized. Even at that distance, Bolan made out the scarred face of the tall figure hurrying from the elevator. With the help of the firewalls that had turned night into day, the Executioner clearly made out the angry faces of Kuschka and Calhoun.

Bolan ejected the clip from his AK-47, found it empty and slapped a fresh mag home.

The Executioner broke from the force making its move to go below. He saw Kuschka and Calhoun race between two sheets of fire and disappear for a moment. Then he saw them heading for what was left of the motor pool in the distance.

Bolan picked it up, determined not to let his prey get away.

21

Bolan, crouched and fanning the killzone with his assault rifle, swiftly angled across the runway. It was as complete a destruction of the enemy complex aboveground as could have been planned for.

It wasn't over.

He raised Grimaldi, his AK-47 ready to cut loose on anything that moved his way or rose up from the dead. It was pretty much down to mop-up detail, at least aboveground. The Hinds were sweeping back and forth, containing their fields of fire to the far south.

Patching through, Bolan told Grimaldi, "I've got a primary-target sighting. I'm moving in on them, just south of what's left of the barracks. Pass the word on to the crew and the other Hinds that I'm a friendly in case they head this way."

"Roger that, Rogue Force. A heartfelt good luck. Nail the bastards."

"I'll be in touch, Lone Eagle. Over and out."

The Executioner darted into the graveyard of flaming wreckage and smoking rubble, a stinking, smoke-shrouded lake of strewed bodies. He saw them in the distance, thirty yards or so ahead, and closing. Incredibly several vehicles had been spared the brunt of the air attack. Shadows ahead of Bolan were momentarily concealed by drifting smoke, licking flames and twisted sheets of wreckage.

Bolan put more distance between himself and the Russian commandos securing the northern descent to the underground complex. No one had noticed his sudden departure, or perhaps they were too busy laying it on the enemy. Either way, he left the commando force to the grim task of securing the belowground complex, confident that they could move down, chop the enemy up in a pincer attack, seize the weapons factory.

The Executioner was locked on to a single goal. He had come too far, killed too many of the enemy, thwarted too many warped dreams to lose his chance now to nail the two men responsible for so much death and suffering.

The Executioner went hunting.

Beyond a firewall Bolan heard the engines of two getaway vehicles already revving to life. He spotted Kuschka, the ex-KGB killer set to bolt, the tall Russian clambering into the cab of an APC, snarling at Calhoun, who pointed to the back of the vehicle and told his three men to pile in.

Bolan surged out from between two tongues of fire and opened up with his AK-47. He went for Calhoun's men first, since they were caught in the open. They were running down the port side of the APC when Bolan's stream of 7.62 mm lead pinned them to the side of the vehicle, bullets chewing them up to dancing scarlet sieves before they crumpled to boneless sprawls. Bolan adjusted his aim, saw Kuschka poke his head out the window, then the vehicle lurched ahead.

Two hardmen who had secured a military-style

jeep, meant to be the rearguard, no doubt, for Kuschka, burst from the vehicle with assault rifles, drawing target acquisition on the big shadow who had come out of nowhere.

Before they even got off the first round, Bolan had fired a long rattling burst from the Kalashnikov, striking them both in the chest and knocking them off their feet.

Bolan plucked two clips off the corpses, then he piled into the jeep, put it in gear and headed in pursuit.

CALHOUN'S BRAIN pulsed with mindless rage. A film of red seemed to obscure his vision. From the shotgun seat, as Kuschka bounced them down a dirt trail that cut through the foothills, Calhoun saw the headlights of the jeep in his side mirror. Their pursuer was a good hundred yards behind them, but Calhoun didn't have to see the face of their hunter to know who it was.

Their nemesis.

Calhoun turned his head, bared his teeth at Kuschka. "So, we're running again, my Russian friend? What's the plan? All my men are dead, so it's just you and me against the fucking problem that shows up again at a complex I would've sworn you said was so secure and remote—"

"Enough with your whining! We would have been annihilated had we stayed put belowground. Be grateful we have this last chance to lure our nameless enemies out here into these hills where we can finish them off."

"Lure them? Maybe you don't know it yet, but all we've been all along is the goddamn bait on a hook, and they've done nothing but chomp down the whole time, taking one big bite here, one there." Calhoun wrapped his fist around the AK-47, noting Kuschka's own assault rifle was leaning against the Russian's leg. Calhoun knew he was finished with the Russian, all his dreams of wealth and nailing down his own small Third World country going up in the flames of the compound they were putting behind them. But he'd find a way out of Russia somehow. Regroup, reorganize, put some money in his pocket. He still had contacts in certain countries hostile to the West. He could always wheel and deal some weapons, train one man's army of freedom fighters. Whatever it took.

Calhoun caught something he didn't trust at all in Kuschka's narrowing gaze, some flicker of madness. "Is this where I get the old 'there's bad news, and then there is very bad news,' Comrade?"

Kuschka actually grinned, reaching between his legs. "No. For you, it is all very bad news."

The barrel of the AK-47 snagged on the dashboard and before he could fully swing up the assault rifle, Calhoun saw the flame leaping from the Makarov's snout. It felt as if the wind were being hammered again and again from his lungs as the bullets slammed into Calhoun's ribs, lancing instant fire that torched every nerve in his body.

BOLAN CUT THE GAP to less than a hundred yards, the headlights of the jeep locking on and flickering all over the APC. He jounced over the uneven terrain of the wide trail, but he was gaining ground. A plan was forming in his mind, one where he could find a way to roll up to the APC's starboard, make a leap for the transport bed and take it from there when the starboard door opened and a body tumbled to the trail.

The figure rolled up near the base of a rock wall, then somehow staggered to its feet, clutching its blood-soaked side. The man was framed by the headlights, and Bolan saw the pain and hate on Calhoun's face. Kuschka had obviously snapped, shot his onetime ally and kicked him out the door. The why of it all didn't matter to Bolan.

Calhoun was still alive and kicking, the former Special Forces major lifting his AK-47 and going for broke. For a heartbeat the soldier made eye contact with Calhoun as his enemy was pinned in the headlights. Then Bolan floored it, had just enough room on the trail to angle for his enemy without slamming into the wall of rock that loomed to his side.

The AK-47 blazed for a moment, jumping around in Calhoun's fists, some mindless bellow of rage and doom reaching Bolan's ears before the slugs blasted in the windshield. The soldier ducked the hail of glass, heard the slugs whining off the hood. The Executioner glanced up over the steering wheel, just in time to catch the snarling mask of Calhoun rushing straight at him before he made impact.

There was a loud thud of flesh yielding to metal, the wheel shuddering in Bolan's grasp, then Calhoun was airborne, hurtled far ahead of the jeep. Before he could correct his course, the soldier felt the tires roll over Calhoun. A crunch of bone in his ears, and Bolan put Calhoun out of mind and lifted the AK-47. He slapped out the jagged teeth of glass with the assault rifle's barrel. Squinting against the wind, he triggered the assault rifle one-handed. He was aiming low, going for the tires, winging bullets off the ground, closing on the APC's rear when the vehicle sluiced, jerked to braking, stopping at an angle that blocked the trail.

The Executioner saw it coming. Maybe Kuschka was tired of running, maybe Kuschka knew it was all over but the dying or maybe the Russian's mind was tweaked with mindless rage and fear. Whatever, the guy was going to make a solitary grandstand attempt.

Bolan hit the brakes, took in the jumble of rock off to the side of the trail, factored that in for cover, a point of attack. He rammed a fresh clip into the AK-47 and burst out the door as Kuschka disappeared from his sight, somewhere inside the cab. A door opened, and Kuschka landed on the far side.

Crouched, Bolan saw the boots on the starboard side, outlined in the headlights. He squeezed the trigger, aiming for the legs, and was rewarded by a sharp howl of pain. Kuschka went down, hidden for a moment behind the starboard rear wheel.

Silence filled the gorge. Bolan wasn't leaving anything to chance and headed into the open, suspecting Kuschka was about to come flying around the rear of the APC.

An animal-like howl of rage hit the air, then the Russian limped into Bolan's sight, holding back on the trigger of his AK-47, spraying the jeep with wild autofire. Scurrying away from Kuschka's tracking line of bullets, Bolan unloaded his assault rifle before Kuschka figured it out and could correct his aim. The Executioner stitched Kuschka crotch to sternum, rode out the recoil and let the line of slugs go high, all but obliterating the scarred visage. No Kevlar would save Kuschka this time.

Slowly Bolan walked up on the twitching form stretched out before him, just to make sure.

The Executioner confirmed his kill.

Bolan heard Grimaldi raising him and lifted the handheld radio.

"Gaylov just informed me the strike force has secured the complex belowground, Rogue Force. We're clear here. I'm on the way. What's happening on your end?"

"Prime targets eliminated, Lone Eagle. I'll be standing by for evac."

Bolan signed off and stood there in the darkness and the silence. Far to the south a peal of thunder rocked the night. The soldier turned, saw the flames shooting for the sky. From that direction the sky appeared to glow, on fire.

For a fleeting moment he wondered about the final conflagration. Would the sky look like that when the final madness gripped humankind?

Bolan discarded the vision as quickly as it flickered through his mind. As long as he had something to say about it, the good ones would always stand against evil and fight that day off.

James Axler

OUTLANDERS™

HELLBOUND FURY

Kane and his companions find themselves catapulted into an alternate reality, a parallel universe where the course of events in history is dramatically different. What hasn't changed, however, is the tyranny wrought by the Archons on mankind...this time, with human "allies."

Book #1 in the new Lost Earth saga, a trilogy that chronicles our heroes' paths through three very different alternate realities...where the struggle against the evil Archons goes on....

THE LOST EARTH SAGA

BOOK 1

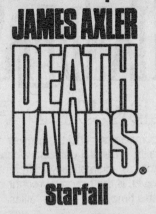

Shadow THE EXECUTIONER®
as he battles evil for 352 pages of
heart-stopping action!

SuperBolan®

#61452	DAY OF THE VULTURE	$5.50 U.S.	☐
		$6.50 CAN.	☐
#61453	FLAMES OF WRATH	$5.50 U.S.	☐
		$6.50 CAN.	☐
#61454	HIGH AGGRESSION	$5.50 U.S.	☐
		$6.50 CAN.	☐
#61455	CODE OF BUSHIDO	$5.50 U.S.	☐
		$6.50 CAN.	☐
#61456	TERROR SPIN	$5.50 U.S.	☐
		$6.50 CAN.	☐

(limited quantities available on certain titles)

TOTAL AMOUNT	$	
POSTAGE & HANDLING	$	
($1.00 for one book, 50¢ for each additional)		
APPLICABLE TAXES*	$	_____
TOTAL PAYABLE	$	_____
(check or money order—please do not send cash)		

To order, complete this form and send it, along with a check or money order for the total above, payable to Gold Eagle Books, to: **In the U.S.:** 3010 Walden Avenue, P.O. Box 9077, Buffalo, NY 14269-9077; **In Canada:** P.O. Box 636, Fort Erie, Ontario, L2A 5X3.

Name: _____

Address: _____ City: _____

State/Prov.: _____ Zip/Postal Code: _____

*New York residents remit applicable sales taxes.
 Canadian residents remit applicable GST and provincial taxes.

GSBBACK1